COVI
The Seventh Day S
By Leslie S

Copyright 2020, Leslie Swartz

Library of Congress Control Number: 2020917129

ISBN: 9798681557517

Happiness is not found in things you possess, but in what you have the courage to release.

William Butler Yeats

Prologue

Tituba placed her infant daughter inside the circle of white candles, the moonlight peeking through the trees cascading its approving glow on the baby's smiling face. She sat on her knees, confident in the protection the forest provided, far away from the prying eyes of the townspeople that would hang her if they knew what she was. She placed her hand on Violet's head and said the words, quietly, but with conviction. "Ne agnosceretur sicut pythonissam." The child giggled as Tituba smiled down at her, relieved that it was done. She bent down and whispered into her daughter's ear, "You will remember this spell. Teach it to your children and your children's children so your generations will always be protected."

She blew out the candles and placed them back in the hollowed-out tree stump she used for hiding spellbooks and ingredients, covering it with rocks before gathering her newborn in her arms.

"Tituba," a voice whispered in the dark.

"Who's there?" She froze, every muscle in her body tense as she clutched the baby to her chest. She scanned the trees and saw the figure of a girl fast approaching.

"It's me, Sarah."

"Oh!" She let out a sigh of relief. "You gave me quite the fright. What are you doing out here at this hour, child? If your father catches you, he'll string you up and me along with you."

"I need to ask you something and I didn't want anyone else to hear."

"All right, well, spit it out, girl. It's late and we need to get you home."

She looked back to make sure she wasn't followed before speaking again. "I need your help. You know, *magic help*."

"Now I *know* you're trying to get me hanged."

"I'm serious, Tituba, please. My mother practiced the craft and she said if I ever needed something, that you were the only person I could go to."

She gently bounced the baby as she closed her eyes, remembering her friend, the girl's mother, who'd recently passed from the pox. "What is it that you want, child?"

"I want you to bring her back. Her and my sister. Bring them back before my father dies of a broken heart."

Tituba's expression turned dark as she stared into the teenager's eyes. "You know I can not."

"Why not?" Sarah whined. "I heard Goody Sawyer talking to her cousin last week and she said--"

"You listen to me, girl," she snapped. "Goody Sawyer is not the same as me. What she does is dark and dangerous and will not result in a happy family reunion. Life and death are not interchangeable. Once a soul has reached its next destination, there is no retrieving it. Not for *us*, anyway. To try is an invitation for wickedness, do you understand?"

She crossed her arms, her lips pouted.

"You stay far away from Goody Sawyer, do you hear me?"

"You can't tell me what to do. You're just a slave."

She scowled. "Little girl, I may be a slave, but I am not *your* slave. You will speak to me respectfully unless you want me to tell your father I found you out at this hour."

"You wouldn't. You'd have to explain why *you* were out."

She laughed. "I have a new baby. Babies cry. Sometimes, a walk in the fresh night air is the only thing that settles them. No one would question why *I* was out of bed at this hour."

"Fine. I'll stay away from Goody Sawyer."

"Good. Just get this out of your head, now. I know you've been put through the mill, but you have to accept life for what it is."

Sarah dropped her arms. "What's that?"

The witch kissed the top of her baby's head, her gaze still fixed on the girl. "Tragic with blinding flashes of beautiful happiness."

"If Tituba won't help me, I will help myself," Sarah whispered as she snuck into Goody Sawyer's bedroom through an open window. She quickly searched the room, making sure to put things back the way she'd found them before moving on to another drawer or cabinet. It was no use. There was nothing there that could help her. Crushed, she walked back to the window, resigned to her defeat. But, as she lifted a leg to climb back out, a floorboard creaked. She backed up and knelt down, lifting the board. Her eyes lit up at the discovery of a leather-bound book with a strange symbol on the front: a square with a vertical line cutting through the center of an X. She opened it to find page after page of chants, lists of ingredients, and odd symbols. "A spellbook," she muttered. She shoved the small book into her reticule, replaced the floorboard, and hopped out the window, hastily making her way to the woods to begin her studies.

The other girls laughed while Sarah used a stick to carve an inverted pentagram in the soft soil of the forest floor. All, except one.

"I think this is a bad idea," Elizabeth blurted as Sarah placed candles at each of the points. She began to light them, dismissing her friend's concerns.

"It's harmless, Lizzie. The book says I can summon him here and make him do my bidding. As long as we don't break the circle, he can't harm us."

Temperance took one last bite of her apple before tossing it to the ground. "I bet nothing happens at all."

"I hope you're right," Elizabeth said, nervously twirling her hair.

"It makes no difference what you think, as long as you recite the words exactly. The book says, 'Five voices speaking as one'. Do you all remember it?" The girls nodded, taking each other's hands around the symbol. "All right. Let's begin. Emergo nunc survus. Emergo nunc servus." The others joined in the chant, repeating the phrase over and over. After several minutes of nothing happening, Elizabeth let go.

"This is pointless."

"I agree," Temperance said, folding her arms. "The sun will set soon. We should get back."

"Please," Sarah begged. "Just a few more minutes." But, the girls were bored, letting go of each other's hands and casting pitiful glances her way.

"I'm sorry, Sarah," Caroline said, already walking away.

Ruth followed her. "Me, too, Sarah. I almost thought it might work."

Temperance patted Sarah's shoulder before joining the others.

"I'm sorry for your loss," Elizabeth told her. "But, it's probably for the best he didn't come. Any gifts given by the Devil would surely come at a price." She, too, left the clearing, leaving Sarah alone to hide what they'd been doing. She blew out the candles and hid them in the hollowed-out tree trunk before smoothing over the dirt, wiping out any trace of the symbol she'd drawn there just a few minutes before. She sat on the ground, head in hands as she wiped away a stray tear. Suddenly, she heard a twig snap. She popped her head up, hoping her friends had returned to try the spell again.

"Are you back?" But, no one answered. She stood, peeking through the trees in the direction of the sound of rustling leaves. "Hello?" When no response came, she turned to retrieve her bag but was stopped in her tracks by a vision of pure evil. It was a figure of a man, except it had no face, no clothes, and no color. It was as if a shadow had come to life. It stood before her, ominous and solid as the trees that surrounded her. Her hand flew to her chest as she struggled to get her breath, her heart beating so fast, she thought it would explode. As she looked over the strange figure, she whispered to herself, "It worked."

"I heard your call," the shadow hissed, its voice little more than a low growl.

"Can you bring my mother and sister back?" she blurted.

The figure tilted its head as dozens of snakes seemed to appear from nowhere, slithering over her shoes and around her ankles. She didn't scream, determined to remain in control of the situation. She ignored the creatures, steadying her breathing as the shadow drew closer. "That is your request?"

"Yes." She swallowed hard as the figure towered over her, the smell of rotted eggs emanating from it as it seemed to grow in size.

"I will do as you ask," it snarled. "But, what you want requires a sacrifice. The blood of a child. Bring me a child, and you will have what you desire." And, with that, it was gone. The snakes disappeared and Sarah was left with a decision to make.

Meanwhile, in the woods, the girls hurried to get home before dark. Caroline and Ruth skipped arm-in-arm while Temperance and Elizabeth followed. Elizabeth kept her head down as she walked, guilt creeping into her thoughts.

"Is it terrible that I'm glad nothing happened?"

"Terrible?" Temperance asked. "I don't think so. The Devil is *not* someone to toy with. Truth be told, though, I think it's all nonsense and superstition. Tituba is a slave deluding herself into thinking she has some control over her circumstances. Goody Sawyer is just bored."

"I hope that's true." They continued to walk as the sun got lower in the sky, carefree, having no reason to think they were in any danger. But, seeping up out of the earth appeared four dark figures. The stench of sulfur surrounded them as they slithered along the forest floor, each attaching itself to one of the girls. They screamed, the demons' touch like fire against their skin. The shadowy figures climbed up the girls' bodies as they tried to run, but the weight of the entities pulled them down to the ground as they covered them entirely. The shadows sank in, absorbing through their new hosts' skin, filling every organ, every cell with their wretched, foul essence.

They rose, wicked grins spreading across the faces of those who used to be Sarah's friends. They ran their hands over their new bodies, delighting in the flesh and the feeling of air moving through their noses and lungs. It had been ages since any of them had been on Earth and they were ready to have some fun.

Once in town, the demons went wild, pulling people's hair, tipping over wagons, and killing a horse with their bare hands. The townspeople fled, hiding in their homes and storm cellars, sure the girls had been possessed by the Devil. The four danced in the street, lifting their dresses over their heads and cackling.

"Such a spectacle," a voice came from the shadows. "You really should learn a bit of discretion. I had no trouble finding you at all."

"Jailer!" the one occupying Temperance howled. "You will not take us back!"

"But, I will," Lucifer said, stepping into the last light of the day. "I always do."

They ran, the one occupying Elizabeth racing back into the woods while the rest bolted toward the church. Lucifer followed the three into the building, shaking his head in derision. "It never ceases to amaze me how unimaginably stupid you demons are. You were out in the open. You could have scattered, maybe saved yourselves. But, you *chose* to be trapped. What was the logic in that decision? Baffling."

They backed away, their eyes wide with fear. "Leave us be, Lucifer!" the one in Ruth screeched. "We won't go with you!"

"Well," he smirked. "Not willingly, I imagine." He rushed them, placing a hand on one of their heads. But, before he could expel the demon, the others began fighting back, hitting him with Bibles and biting at his arms and chest. He rolled his eyes. "Fine. We'll do this the quick way, then." He slammed one demon onto the floor and tore its intestines out, blood spurting from its mouth and nose. He snapped another's neck and grabbed the last one by the hair, pulling it back and looking into its eyes. "As I said, I'll *always* take you back." He plunged his hand into the demon's chest and yanked out its heart, tossing it aside as the body fell. When all three demons had slipped out of their hosts and slithered their way back to their cages, Lucifer turned, sighing with regret to see a handful of parishioners hiding between the pews. He thought about addressing them, explaining what had happened, but there was still a demon out there and he had no time for coddling a few frightened humans. He left the church, on his way to finish the task at hand.

Back in the woods, the demon residing in Elizabeth became hysterical. It clawed at the ground, desperate to dig a hole big enough to hide in until Lucifer moved on, tricked into thinking it had kept running.

"Elizabeth?" Tituba called, coming upon her as she gathered evening primrose. "What are you doing out here in the dark?"

"Never you mind," the demon seethed, not looking up from its work.

The faint scent of sulfur hit Tituba's nose as she stopped, dropping her flower basket and gasping.

"Move along, witch," the demon hissed, still digging.

"I won't," she said, instead running up on the demon, grasping it by the head and yelling, "Apage ire in domum suam!"

Its eyes flew open wide as the inky shadow slowly tore away, sliding down to the ground and disappearing into the grass.

"Well, it looks as though you've done my job for me," Lucifer said. "I'm impressed. And, what might your name be, love?"

"Tituba Indian. And, you are?"

"Irrelevant, it would seem. Gratitude. Your assistance is much appreciated."

"Tituba?" the girl breathed, sitting up and rubbing her head. "What happened?"

"You just fainted, girl. Go on home now."

She nodded, getting up and walking away, casting Lucifer a suspicious glance as she passed.

In the distance, they could hear a baby crying. "Violet." Tituba ran toward the sound, Lucifer following out of sheer curiosity. They came to the clearing and there they found Sarah with the infant, stolen from her crib. "What are you doing, girl?"

"I'm sorry," Sarah said through tears. "He said he'd bring them back. I just had to give him…" She looked down at the crying child's face. "I have to."

"Subsisto," Tituba ordered, causing the girl to freeze where she stood. She took her baby back, rocking her as her crying quieted. "Who told you to do this?"

The girl was immobile but for her eyes and mouth. Fresh tears came as she said the words, "The Devil."

Lucifer guffawed.

Tituba gawked at him. "Why is that funny?"

He composed himself, unable to keep from smiling. "I can assure you, the Devil told her no such thing. He does not take children as payment for favors. The idea of it is absurd."

"It's true," Sarah insisted. "He--" She stopped, the egg smell returning. Snakes rose from the grass, slithering over their feet, wrapping themselves around their ankles as even the fireflies seemed to flee in panic.

The dark figure began to take form in front of them as Lucifer's expression turned cold. "Moloch."

"Take her," Tituba said, handing the baby to Lucifer.

"Take her? Are you so trusting? I am a stranger to you."

She looked into his eyes, seeing in a way others could not. "I have nothing to fear from you, Bringer of Light. Others may fear you, but I see your heart." She scurried to the hollowed-out tree trunk and rifled through books, candles, and potions. Finally, she got to a small, bronze statue of a man with the head of a cow, its seven chambers wide open.

"I should be fighting this beast, not babysitting. You have no idea what you're up against."

She gave him a condescending smile before setting her gaze on the figure. "Capti sunt vobis." The beast bellowed pained screams into the night as it was blown apart, reduced to ash, and sucked wailing into the statue. "Cinccino." The chambers locked, trapping the monster inside. She placed the statue back in the trunk, this time waving a hand over it, reciting the words, "Operimentum lutum," as dirt sprung from the ground, covering the trunk in two feet of earth.

Lucifer stared in awe, fascinated by the power this witch possessed. "Your mother's a force of nature," he whispered to the baby in his arms. "Perhaps, you'll grow up one day to be just as skilled. For the sake of humanity, I hope that you do." The child giggled and he smiled, finding a moment of peace in the infant's blissful ignorance.

"As for you," Tituba scolded, turning her attention back to Sarah. "What you did tonight was unforgivable. You can no longer be trusted with the power of speech. I am sorry, but I can not risk you doing something this feeble again. I must take your words, if for no other reason than to protect my daughter from your rampant stupidity."

"No!" Sarah yelped. "Tituba, please! I'm sorry!"

"Nec ultra addas loqui."

The girl mouthed the word 'please', but no sound came from her throat. She stared in horror at Tituba's stoic face, pleading with her eyes to give her voice back.

"Iam moveri," Tituba said, releasing the girl from her frozen position. She put her hand to her throat, silently screaming as tears streamed down her freckled cheeks. She ran away, leaving Tituba to take her daughter from Lucifer, bouncing her as she sighed. "I did not enjoy doing that."

"Yes, well, it needed doing," he told her. "That girl is a fool and would no doubt dabble in more things of which she has no business. I'd venture to say you did her a favor."

She looked him over, squinting as she made her assessment. "You and I are cut from the same cloth, I think."

He laughed. "My dear woman, you have no idea how wrong you are about that." But, as he walked her home, he couldn't help but feel a strange connection; a spark of hopeful peace between them. He could have been wrong, but if he wasn't mistaken, what he was feeling was the beginnings of friendship.

Chapter 1

Her scent was like oxygen as Will breathed her in, the sweet vanilla on her skin enveloping his senses as he kissed her neck and shoulder. Michelle moved beneath him, her hands on his back as their legs intertwined. Her breathing quickened as she climaxed, the feeling of air moving so quickly through her lungs frightening her as she hadn't experienced the sensation in months. When they were finished, he rolled to his side of the bed and her hand flew to her chest as she felt her heart beating much more rapidly than before.

"Something's wrong with me," she panted, sitting up.

He sprung up next to her and put a hand on her back. "What?"

"I don't know. I feel," her hand slid down to her lower abdomen. "I have to go to the bathroom. I have to go to the *bathroom*?" She got up and went to the restroom. A minute later, she came back, hands still wet from washing. Her eyes were like saucers as she held her stomach, her heart beating out of her chest. "I went to the bathroom."

"Uh, congratulations?"

She rolled her eyes. "*Vampires don't pee, Will.*" She went to the window and tentatively slipped her hand between it and the blackout curtains. The sun had come up just a few minutes before and its light should have cooked her skin like meat under a broiler, but it didn't. She pulled it back and looked at it, the shock on her face causing Will to stand. She looked at him, eyes wild, before pulling the curtain back and standing directly in front of the glass. Again, nothing happened. She was fine. "What the fuck?"

"Kinda giving the neighbors a show."

"Look at me!" She spun around, a cautious smile curling her lips.

"Oh, I'm looking," he said, putting his hand to his chin.

"Look outside, Will. It's *day!*"

As the post-coital fog lifted from his brain, he finally understood. "Are you…"

"GABRIEL!" she shouted, throwing a tee-shirt on and racing from their room to the angel's.

"What fresh hell?" Gabriel complained, rubbing her eyes and sitting up in bed.

"What am I?"

She gagged. "Oh, my Christ. You smell like semen. Please get out of here with that shit. You're gonna give me nightmares."

"That's my bad," Will said, buttoning his jeans as he joined them.

"I know it's your bad. That's my problem. You two really need your own place. This is not okay. Move into Tae's. It's just sitting there."

"Gabriel," Michelle bubbled, sitting in front of her on the bed.

She huffed, "I'm gonna have to burn this blanket."

"*What am I?*"

She folded her arms. "What do you me--" She stopped, tilting her head as it became clear. "Holy shit." She leaped out of bed, the strap of her satin nightgown falling off her shoulder. She replaced it and banged on the bathroom door where her girlfriend was taking a shower. "WENDY!"

Allydia basked in the early-morning sun, allowing herself to feel the warmth of it for the first time in thousands of years. The cool, early-fall air blew in through the open window, waking Wyatt from a dreamless sleep. She inhaled deeper than she had in millennia, not out of habit or emotional reaction, but because she needed to. She closed her eyes, her mind calm, and her soul at peace.

"What are you doing?" he asked, getting out of bed and standing behind her.

She smiled as he wrapped his arms around her. "Breathing."

"You have goosebumps."

She laughed, inspecting her arm. "I do! I don't know that that's ever happened before."

He kissed the side of her head and gazed out the window overlooking the courtyard as he rested his chin on her shoulder. "How do you feel?"

She rubbed his arm and stared up into the bright, cloudless sky. "Like myself. I feel more like myself than I have since the night I died. I am worried, though."

"About what?"

She closed the window and turned to face him, biting her lip and looking up at him with fear in her eyes. "I'm human now. Nothing special. The pheromones are gone. What if you come to discover that without them, you don't want me anymore?"

He tucked her hair behind her ear and touched her cheek. "First, human doesn't mean not special. You don't need superpowers to hold my interest and I definitely don't have to be drugged to want you." He took her face in his hands. "I love you…full stop. No more separations. No more doubts. It's me and you…the end, okay?"

She nodded and he kissed her, sliding his hands down her neck and shoulders. She pulled away and gasped, her hand flying to her stomach.

"What?" he asked.

"I'm hungry," she giggled. Her smile broadened. "Wyatt, I'm hungry! I can eat *food*!" She ran past him, making a beeline for the kitchen as he chuckled and followed. She stood in front of the open fridge pulling random things from it, having no idea what any of it tasted like or what ingredients went together. She gathered kiwi's, an orange, a block of cheddar, and two steaks. "What can I make with this?"

He laughed, taking the items and putting them back where they'd come from. "Nothing good if you mixed them all together." He gestured to the island. "Sit down, I'll make you something. What did you like to eat before?"

She sat. "Lentil soup, a lot of fruit. My favorite thing was flatbread I made with barley flour and water. I may still remember how to do it. Do you think I could find a millstone in working condition?"

"A *millstone*? I doubt it." He poured her a glass of orange juice and placed a kiwi in a bowl, cutting it in half and handing her a spoon. "Why don't you snack on that while I make some eggs and toast?"

She took a sip of juice, her eyes lighting up as she set the glass down and smacked her lips.

"What do you think?"

"Tart."

He snickered, placing bread in the toaster and cracking eggs into a pan. She dug her spoon into the flesh of the kiwi and took a bite. She put the spoon down and covered her mouth as she swallowed. He looked over at her as he whisked. "You okay?"

She reached for her juice. "I like the sweet part in the center." She took another sip and put it down, puckering her lips and squeezing her eyes shut. "Is all of your fruit so sour?"

He smiled, taking a banana from the bunch and handing it to her. She looked it over, her eyebrows scrunched. He laughed, taking it and peeling it for her before handing it back. She took a bite, raising her eyebrows in approval.

"Better?"

She nodded emphatically, swallowing, and taking another mouthful. He took two plates from the cabinet and spooned the scrambled eggs onto them before buttering the freshly popped-up toast. He slid a plate in front of her and handed her a fork before sitting and beginning to eat. She watched him and mimicked his movements, taking a bite of toast, then a forkful of eggs. "This is very good," she told him, pointing to the toast. "It's the butter. It used to take me half an hour to churn butter for the day. Now, you can just buy it. So convenient." They continued eating as he watched her, smiling to himself as he reveled in her happiness. In the entire time he'd known her, he'd never seen her so relaxed, so comfortable in her own skin. *This* was who she truly was and who she was always meant to be.

"Holy crap balls," Wendy said, Michelle's chin in her hand. "I guess I didn't know my own strength."

"What does that mean?" Gabriel asked, joining the others in the kitchen after throwing on a tee-shirt and pair of jeans.

"To do the spell to cure Allydia, I needed more power, so I absorbed my dead great-aunt's. She left it to me, it was purely consensual. Apparently, I didn't just take away Allydia's vampirism, I took away vampirism all together." She cringed, hoping no one would be too upset with her. "I feel really bad. I didn't mean to like, commit genocide."

"Did I hear 'genocide'?" Lucifer asked, emerging from his room, looking like a men's magazine cover model somehow first thing in the morning.

Gabriel threw him an orange.

"Thank you."

"She accidentally made all the vampires human."

"She did? Well done, Wendy, though I don't think that counts as proper genocide. Mutilation, maybe. We should celebrate. Perhaps young William can make us all a decent breakfast?"

Michelle's ears perked up. "Oh, my God, I've missed bacon so hard."

Will laughed. "On it."

Yo, B, Gabriel thought.

Yeah? He responded.

There's something Dia needs to know.

Chapter 2

The crow perched itself on the fire escape as Julia searched inside, rifling through drawers and looking over stacks of mail. She looked over the envelopes, the corner of her lip turning up in a satisfied smirk. "Wendy." Her locator spell had led her to this apartment, but the resident was nowhere to be found. She did, however, find the broken Catseye lying haphazardly on the floor, clearly discarded after its contents were purged. There was still a bit of blood smeared on its edge, a handy ingredient, so she pocketed the necklace and continued to look for anything else that might prove useful. As she opened the hall closet, she felt her sisters enter the building. She rushed to find anything else that might be of use, hoping to find something that would give her a clue about where the mystery witch might be, who her friends were, or where she worked. But, all she found in the closet were towels, blankets, and, sitting on the floor, a large trunk with a heavy-duty padlock. She knelt and held her hand over the metal lock. "Patefacio sursum." The lock broke and fell to the floor just as the other witches opened the door and came into the apartment. They were all there, the six remaining witches of her coven, not including Poe, who she was still livid about letting slip through her fingers. She stood to greet them, knowing full well the punishment she was about to receive. If Libby's message hadn't made it to them, Poe surely had. She would be marked a traitor, banned from coven gatherings of any kind for at least a month but up to a year while she proved her loyalty, doing menial spells and any other grunt work the coven deemed necessary. Her hope was that she could find this Wendy on her own and deliver her to the elders, thereby ensuring her place as not only a member of the coven but as its new leader.

"Julia," Donna said, stepping out in front of the others, all with their arms crossed, cold stares on each of their faces. "What have you found?"

"Nothing, yet," she lied. "Just this trunk. I just got the lock off."

"It's time for you to go, not just from this place, but from the coven."

"What? What do you mean?"

"We know what you did to Libby. We know that you corrupted two of our sisters. Your actions got *them* killed, as well. There is no redemption for what you've done."

"You don't understand. I was just trying to find Grace's magic. It belongs to us! I was just--"

"Enough," Donna boomed, her voice rattling the windows and causing a gust of wind to blow Julia's long red hair off her shoulders. "You have betrayed your coven, a crime from which there is no coming back."

"But--"

"Julia, you are shunned." They turned their backs to her, keeping their eyes on the wall as they waited for her to leave. Her stomach dropped, their abandonment like a death. She held a shaky hand to her diaphragm as she tried to steady her breathing, the loss like a kick to the chest. Tears puddled in her eyes as she made her way to the door. From the hall, she looked back at them, their eyes still averted. Donna began to close the door, leaving enough of an opening that Julia could still hear her. "If your thoughts turn to revenge, remember that we still have your measure."

The door slammed, leaving Julia truly alone for the first time in her life. She wiped her tears and took the Catseye from her pocket, rage replacing hurt as she put it back, more determined than ever to make Grace's magic her own.

Inside, Donna went to the trunk, opening it to find Wendy's supplies: Goofer dust, grave dirt, candles, a variety of crystals and herbs, and at the bottom, wrapped in a linen cloth, was a spellbook. She opened the leather-bound book, its weight heavy and size lumbering. She gasped, her eyes widening, her mouth hanging open.

"A grimoire?" Nicole asked.

"No," Donna said, her voice quivering as she ran her hand over the first page. "A book of shadows."

"Whose?"

She carefully re-wrapped it, gently putting it back where she'd found it. She stood and closed the closet door, her heart racing as she told the others, "Tituba's."

Her words were met with gasps, Nicole dropping the letter she'd picked up to learn the name of the person living there. "Are you serious?"

She steadied herself against the wall and nodded. "Grace said she'd had a sister, but that she died years ago. She never mentioned Eva having children."

"Wendy," Nicole said, picking up the envelope and showing it to her.

"A blood relative. A born-Tituban witch. Someone that can carry the power of her magic without being destroyed by it. Grace didn't *hide* her magic. She chose her heir. She gifted us with a new leader, as powerful as she was, if not more so. This Wendy has Tituba's original spells. All of her knowledge. The things she could teach us! Grace didn't betray us. *She saved us.*"

Julia stood outside the building, cloaked and waiting. After a while of pacing, she spotted Poe hurrying to the entrance. She bolted toward her, but Griffon got to her first, the bird knocking her down and clawing at her face. The girl screamed, trying to shoo it away, but it was relentless, scratching at the skin of her cheeks and forehead, drawing blood as it cawed. It finally flew off as Julia approached, giving Poe the chance to stand up. As she was brushing the street-dust off her pants, Julia grabbed her from behind, wrapping her arms around the girl so tightly, she could barely breathe. Julia snickered. "You're not the only one with a familiar willing to do their bidding. Come on. You and I need to have a chat. Domum." The crow flew over the now empty sidewalk, its talons dripping with blood. It squawked again as it took off in the direction of the place Julia had teleported to, leaving the witches still inside the building none the wiser.

Chapter 3

"Giovanni La Rosa," Navid muttered. After nearly an hour of sifting through hundreds of social media accounts under the name, he finally found the one associated with his father. His profile listed him as being fifty years old, originally from Catania, Sicily, now living and working in Edinburgh. "There you are, Dad." The picture in the profile was unnerving. Navid covered his mouth as he noticed the similarities in their faces. Their cheekbones, smiles, and noses all matched. He felt like he was looking into his own future, one with a black jumper, a glass of red wine, and salt-and-pepper hair. Looking closer, he realized he recognized the restaurant the photo had been taken in. The blue, high-back chairs were a dead giveaway. He'd been there a few years before. He'd had the Cullen skink and a Blood, Smoke, and Sand. Had they crossed paths and never known it?

As he scrolled down the page, he noticed something strange. Every picture on his dad's timeline was of him with a different woman, all beautiful, and all at least twenty years younger than him. The captions read, *With Samantha at the park* and, *Beach day with Ingrid.* In one, he'd written, *Scuba diving with Holly and Sabine,* except they were very obviously in someone's flat and through the window in the background he could see that it was snowing. "Oh, that's just not right." He clicked on the "friends" list and noticed immediately that every person he was following was a gorgeous woman. "At least they're all adults." He closed the laptop and sat back in his chair, staring at the top of the computer like it had offended him somehow. He tapped his fingers on it, mulling over if he should reach out or not. Just as he was about to reopen the computer to run a background check, a knock came on the door. He went to the kitchen and grabbed a butcher knife before opening it. "Oh, hello." He stepped aside, letting a frantic Hartley in and closing the door behind her. "Apologies for the knife," he said, putting it back where he'd gotten it. "Can never be too careful, some of your lot wanting me dead and all."

"Where's the queen?" she asked, stomping through the apartment, poking her head in every room.

"Not here. Said she had somethin' to do last night. Hey, how are you out in the daylight?"

"That was *my* question." She paced the floor, her hands trembling as she checked her phone. "It's dying. Perfect."

"There's a charging station on the kitchen counter. You're free to use it."

"I know where it is." She marched to the kitchen and slammed her phone on the charging pad, trying desperately to control her anxiety. But, her heart felt like it was going a mile a minute and for the first time since the Civil Rights Era, she was sweating. "Look at me," she snapped, opening the fridge, ignoring the blood bags still hanging inside and taking a bunch of grapes. "Look at this crazy shit." She shoved several in her mouth and ate them, dropping the rest onto the counter.

"I'm sorry, miss, but you're gonna have to give me more to go on."

"I'm *human*."

"Ah. I did notice you look a little different. Wasn't gonna say nothin' as not to offend. A little more color in the cheeks. Still very pretty, just a wee less menacing."

"Are you hitting on me?"

"No, oh, God, sorry! I didn't mean to make you uncomfortable."

"You didn't, I just don't think you know…" She folded her arms and squinted as she found the words. "I'm pretty sure you're straight and I'm carrying a little more baggage than the girls you're used to." She looked down at herself and back up at him.

He arched an eyebrow as the front door flew open.

"Hartley, are you all right?" Allydia said, coming in and giving her assistant a once-over. "I tracked your phone. How do you feel?"

"How did this happen?" She looked at her queen, realizing she, too, was no longer a vampire.

"A witch did a spell, removing the original one that turned me. I didn't think it would affect anyone else."

"Well, it did. It affected *everyone else*. Oliver, the diplomats, Phindi, and the rest. We're *all* human."

Navid nodded to his grandmother and went to the living room, giving the women some privacy.

Allydia brushed her assistant's cheek. "You look flushed. Are you hurt?"

"No, I'm just freaking out! I don't know how to be," she waved a hand over the length of her body. "*This*."

"It's an adjustment."

"I'm weak. Look how thin I am! Someone could snap me like a dry twig. How will I survive?"

"Strength isn't in size, Hartley. It's in discipline. If you're concerned about your safety, take a self-defense class. Krav Maga or Jiu-Jitsu."

"I mastered both of those decades ago, at your instruction."

"Oh, that's right. Well, you see then, you have nothing to fear."

"I'm a trans woman in America. I'd be insane *not* to be afraid."

"Then, do as the humans do. Carry mace, don't go out alone after dark, and if someone attacks you, yell 'fire' instead of 'rape' or 'help' because people will be more likely to assist you."

"That's incredibly depressing."

"Yes. We may have been predators in our time, but humans can be the most evil creatures on Earth. You'll have to be careful now, but you will be fine."

She took a deep breath and nodded, taking her phone from the charger and slipping it into her back pocket. "I'll let everyone know."

"Thank you. But, Hartley, I'm no longer your queen. You are free. Do whatever you wish. Live your life the way you see fit. Go to the beach, watch a sunrise. Have fun and be happy."

"I'll try, Your," she stopped herself. "*Allydia*. That'll take some getting used to." She left, feeling only slightly calmer than she had when she'd arrived.

"How are you feeling?" Allydia asked, entering the living room where Navid sat at the computer.

"Better. So, vampires have gone extinct?"

"It would appear so."

"I hate to bring this up, but isn't that exactly what Judas wanted?"

She shot him a look and folded her arms.

"Sorry."

"Have you eaten?"

"Yeah, your angel friend had a boatload of groceries sent over. The freezer in there is full of ice cream in flavors I've never heard of. One has a picture of a late-night chat show host on the package with bits of waffle cone already mixed in. It's incredible. Remind me to thank her properly if I ever see her again."

She gave him a knowing look.

"What?"

"Even if she wasn't taken, she would never be good enough for you."

"What are you on about? I wasn't..."

She raised her eyebrows.

"And what do you mean, 'not good enough'? She's a bloody angel. There's literally nothing better than that."

"Gabriel isn't a *bad* person, she's just...preoccupied. Her loyalty is to her Father. Her siblings come second and while I can tell she holds a deep affection for the woman she's seeing, she will always be last on her list of priorities. God's Messenger will always put her duty first. As it should be, of course, but you deserve to be someone's whole world."

"That's sweet of you to say, Gran, but--"

"Did you just call me 'Gran'?"

"Uh, yeah, sorry. It just seems disrespectful to call you by your given name, seein' as how you're my ancestor and all. Is it too weird?"

"It's a little weird."

"Right, yeah, sorry."

"I like it, though. It makes me feel important. After giving up my kingdom, it's nice to feel connected to someone, like I matter."

"Of course you matter," he said standing up and looking her in the eye. "Aside from a sleazy womanizing father across the pond, you're the only family I've got. Don't think for a second that you don't matter, especially to me."

She smiled. "Thank you, Navid." She looked behind her in the direction of the kitchen and back at him. "Now, tell me more about this ice cream."

Chapter 4

Poe fought to break free of her mullein prison, but the more she struggled against the thick stalks woven around her, the tighter they became, eventually squeezing so hard around her abdomen that she could hardly breathe.

"Arctius," Julia said, summoning more flowers to bind her arms to her sides. The watchful eyes of the coven would have made interrogating the girl impossible in the city. Now, though, in the seclusion of Grace's cottage in Tarrytown, Julia was free to do what was necessary to get the information she needed, no matter how unpleasant the method may be. "Who's Wendy?"

"Like I'd tell *you*," Poe shot back.

She sighed and folded her arms, tapping her foot on the soft grass. "Bestiola." Scurrying from all directions, thousands of ants, beetles, and spiders made their way to Poe who stood helpless, tangled in a web of yellow and green. They crawled up her legs and over the rest of her body, so many in number that she could hear them as they moved. But, even as her heart pounded in her chest, she remained defiant.

"Bugs?" she mocked. "They're harmless. Your torturing skills are severely lacking, bitch."

Julia furrowed her brow. "Mures inclusi essent."

"Oh, shit," Poe whispered as hundreds of rats burrowed out from underground and sped toward her. They climbed up her legs, the weight of them so heavy that she fell onto her back. They swarmed her, nipping at her nose and earlobes. She tried again to get out of her entanglement, but it was no use. Julia's magic was stronger than hers. "I'll never tell you!" she shouted through the deafening squeaks of the earth-covered rats. "You'll never find her!"

Julia's patience had worn thin. She watched as the vermin ate away at the girl's skin, tapping her fingers on her arm as she pondered her next move. "Nice of you to join," she said as the crow landed on the fence to her left. It squawked as if in response and fluttered its wings. "If she won't talk, should I just kill her?" It squawked again. "That's what I think, too. Arctius." This time, a six-foot stalk curled around Poe's neck, choking the life from her in a slow and steady fashion. "Tell me again how my torturing skills are lacking."

The young witch's heart beat out of control as her face began to turn blue. Her eyes rolled back in her head and the morning sunlight grew dim as consciousness faded. The sound of the rats and insects disappeared. Even her heartbeat, which was like thunder in her ears a moment before was gone, replaced by the sound of an unfamiliar woman's voice, her heavy German accent making her words almost unintelligible to the girl on the brink of death.

"Wake up, Enkelin," the voice demanded. "This witch can not best you. She is *weak* where *you* are *strong*."

Who are you? she thought. *Am I hallucinating?*

"I am the source of your power, Enkelin. Take all of it, everything I have, and rise up. Become the witch you were meant to be."

Color came back to her face as she gasped for air, the rats and insects fleeing from her as if she were a sinking ship. The flowers, too, loosened and recoiled, freeing her from her floral coffin.

"What the..." Julia muttered.

Poe steadied her breathing as her eyes glowed emerald green, realizing who the mystery voice had belonged to, the words slipping from her no longer scratchy throat. "Merga Bein." In one quick motion, she was on her feet, her combat boots sinking into the soil farther than they should have for a girl as slight as she.

Julia looked on in horror as Poe stepped toward her, her calm, deliberate movements making her stomach flip. "That's why Grace was so obsessed with you," she panted. "You're a descendant of one of the most powerful witches of all time. She brought you in to strengthen the coven, so she could leave her magic to this Wendy person. Who is she? How is she related to Grace? Where is she?!"

Poe stared, her shimmering eyes causing a lump to form in Julia's throat. She swallowed it, doing her best to appear unafraid...and failing. The young witch raised her arms at her sides and held them there for a moment before clapping her hands together, sending a shock wave in her kidnapper's direction, knocking her back all the way from the garden through the back door of the house. She broke through the screen door and fell onto her back, the window above the sink shattering from the force of the sonic boom. She sat up, giving a puzzled glance to the rabbit sitting on the table looking unbothered as it continued to eat from a food dish. She hurried to her feet and rushed to the living room and out the front door where she found Poe waiting, eyes still sparkling. Julia nearly fell over at the sight of the girl.

"Supernatet," Poe said, her voice like a razor through the air. Julia gasped as she was lifted from the ground, made to hover as Poe moved closer.

The teenager raised her hand, but before she could complete the spell, Julia yelped, "Alio!" and disappeared, teleporting off to who knows where leaving Poe alone with her new-found strength.

Phindi sat uncomfortably in the seat of the plane, the cursed sun mocking her through the small window as she stared ahead, unwilling to give it even a second of her attention. After getting Hartley's call and learning of the queen's abandonment, her remaining soldiers fled from the citadel, excited to begin their new lives as humans. Gifted with the queen's riches, they ventured out on their own, relishing their sudden freedom and bathing in the light of the nearest star that would have broiled them alive not twenty-four hours earlier. They disgusted her, their willingness to let this injustice stand confounding and aggravating her. The fiercest warriors on Earth, now relegated to mediocrity. She was livid, but more than that, she felt betrayed. Hartley had explained that the queen only meant to shackle *herself* to mortality, that the rest of them being dragged into the muck along with her was an accident of an over-zealous witch. But, that made her treachery even worse. She meant to leave them, cast them aside in favor of an ill-conceived human life. *Human.* It was absurd. The longer she sat there, the angrier she became, the mingling smells of the other passengers' meals making her stomach turn. She had no plan for what she'd do when she landed on the queen's doorstep. She hadn't thought it through and was still having trouble forming a cohesive sentence, let alone a plan of action. She only knew she wanted to cause her former queen pain. She wanted to hurt her, directly and with her bare hands. She wanted to make her suffer.

Chapter 5

Wendy opened the door to her apartment to find a group of women waiting for her inside. She could feel their power before she'd entered the building and immediately recognized them as some of the witches that attended her great-aunt's funeral. "Grace's coven," she said, closing the door behind her and dropping her keys on the coffee table.

"How did you know that?" one of them asked. "What am I saying? *Of course,* you knew."

Another stood from her spot on the sofa, trembling as she slowly approached. She was older than the rest as evidenced by her crow's feet and the wisps of gray that framed her face. Wendy was made uncomfortable by the intensity with which the woman stared at her, the hope in her eyes perplexing. "You look just like her."

Wendy took a step back. "Is that why you're staring so hard? Because it's creepy."

"I'm sorry," the woman said, blinking a few times. "You just look so much like Grace. It's uncanny. I'm Donna. This is Nicole, Linda, Ashley, Melissa, and Stephanie."

She looked over the group, all sitting politely with hands folded in their laps, their expressions ranging from shocked to anticipatory. The one called Stephanie, a woman in her early twenties, was visibly shaking while Melissa looked to be on the verge of tears. "Why are you here?"

"We felt Grace's magic and tracked it. We thought we'd find it here, but only the residue remained. Why can't I feel it on you? You're Wendy, Grace's niece, right?"

"Grand-niece. I won't give you her power. It would kill you. I'm sorry, I can feel that you're all powerful witches, but this would definitely leave you a drooling mess."

"Oh, of course, no, we don't want to take it." She looked back at her sisters who gave her an approving nod. She took a shaky breath before addressing her again. "We're asking you to join our coven. Not only join, but lead us as our Priestess."

She scoffed. "You're joking."

Donna looked puzzled. "We found Tituba's book of shadows in your closet. We know how powerful you are."

"You what now?" She stomped to the closet and dug through her belongings until she found the book, flipping through the pages until she was sure it was intact.

"We didn't steal anything," Donna promised.

"We wouldn't dare," She heard Nicole murmur.

She replaced the book and closed the closet door, furrowing her brow as she turned back to look at the women. "You broke in here, went through my stuff, and now you want me to join your coven? What if I hadn't taken Grace's magic into me? If it was still in the Catseye, what would you have done? Steal it? Try to activate it yourselves?"

The ladies shifted in their seats as Donna wrung her hands. "W-w-we'd have done the same thing," she stammered. "Find out who you were and then wait. We are a peaceful coven. We only wanted to know why Grace hid her magic from us. Now, we understand. She left it to a blood relative. It makes perfect sense. She chose you to lead us."

"Lady, I'm not sure she even knew I existed. She probably just wanted to keep you all from getting yourselves killed."

Donna looked hurt by the assertion but held her composure. "Either way, you are the last born-Tituban witch. This coven is yours...if you'll have it."

Wendy sighed. "Listen, guys, you seem like a lovely group of chicks. Maybe a touch Stepford, but aside from the whole breaking-and-entering thing, probably perfectly nice. But, I've never been part of a real coven, let alone been one's Priestess. I can see how important this is to you, but, I'm sorry. I'm not your girl."

Donna's posture straightened and her face went hard. "Very well. Let's go, ladies." She turned and led the others single-file out the door. Tears now flowed down Melissa's cheeks as she took one last look at Wendy before closing the door behind her.

Wendy folded her arms, chewing on her bottom lip as she weighed her options, knowing there really were none. "Son of a bitch." She went into her bedroom and grabbed a suitcase, opening it up and throwing clothes inside. She knew she'd never be safe there now that her identity had been discovered. If Grace's coven didn't attack her, another would. Tituban magic was too tempting. She'd have to abandon the apartment, maybe change her name. She'd have to stay with Gabriel for a few days until she got settled. She'd been spending most nights at her place, anyway. "Shouldn't be a problem."

She whipped her head around at the sudden banging on the front door. She zipped the suitcase and sleuthed to the living room, feeling the immense power coming from the witch waiting in the hall. She looked out the peephole and saw Poe nervously looking behind her. She opened the door and pulled her in, slamming it closed and locking it before heading back to the bedroom where she took another suitcase from the closet and began filling it.

"Hey, Poe. Your coven was just here, rifling through my shit. Looks like I'm going on the lam."

"The coven? Was Julia with them?"

"Who? No, no one named Julia. Donna, Nicole,"

"Are you sure? Julia wasn't here?"

"You okay, Poe? You look flushed. Also, did you get like, nine-thousand times more powerful since the last time I saw you?"

"Probably over nine-thousand. We have to go. *Now.*"

"That's why I'm packing."

"No. *Right now.* Julia just tortured me in my own backyard trying to get information about you. If the coven was here without her, that means she's probably been shunned. They must know about her killing Libby and--"

"Wait, wait, wait. That was a lot of what-the-fuck keywords just then. Torture? Killing? Who's Julia?"

"She's been trying to find Grace's magic. She wanted to take over the coven, but if they kicked her out,"

"She'll want it for herself."

"Exactly." Poe looked out the window to the street, making sure she hadn't been followed. "I tried to warn you about her, but your friend sent me away."

"What friend?"

"The psychic one. Brown hair, fancy boots, knew where I get my magic from. She was here when I came by before. Gave me *a million dollars* so I could get out of town. Probably saved my ass."

Wendy's cheeks went hot. "Would it be okay if I stay with you for a few days?"

"Sure. Are you allergic to rabbits?"

"No."

"Cool. Let's go."

She took Tituba's book of shadows from the closet and shoved it in a suitcase before zipping it. "I just have a stop to make first."

Gabriel laughed out loud. "Over nine-thousand. That's *hysterical*."

Wendy stormed into her girlfriend's apartment, Poe trailing behind, carrying both suitcases.

"Wendy," Lucifer greeted from the couch, putting his newspaper down. "Who's your friend?"

Wendy leaned against the island and crossed her arms. "Poe, Lucifer. Lucifer, Poe."

Poe dropped the luggage. "Not like *Lucifer,* Lucifer, right?"

"The one and only," he smirked.

"Holy shit."

"You're mad," Gabriel said, pushing Wendy's hair behind her ear. She smacked her hand away.

"Yeah, I'm mad. You should have told me about Julia when you found out. She tortured Poe. You should have--"

"My brother died that night!" Gabriel shot back, her eyes widening in anger and confusion. "I couldn't handle it if something happened to you. I was trying to protect you."

"I don't need protection. I've been taking care of myself for a long time. You shouldn't have hidden it from me."

"Like you hid New Zealand? Or your side hustle as a one-stop-shop problem solver for witches? You lied to protect yourself. How can you be mad when *I* was trying to protect you, *too*?"

"That was *my* secret to keep. This is different. People have died. Poe almost died. More people could *die*."

"Yeah, people like *you*! After what happened to Cam, I couldn't risk it."

"I'm sorry about your brother, you know I am. But, you can't hide things from me, especially witch stuff. I know it's not saving-the-world shit like you're used to, but it *is* life and death. So, I'm gonna go figure out how to deal with this Julia thing, and then…I don't know."

"You don't know about what?"

She pursed her lips. "Us. I need some time to think." She spun on her heel and left the apartment, Poe picking up the bags and scurrying behind.

"That was a bit melodramatic," Lucifer said, getting up and walking to the door, closing it as he looked back at his sister who'd gone pale, her lip quivering as she stared into nothing. "Sister," He hesitantly moved closer as he noticed the blender and toaster beginning to shake on the counter. Her breathing quickened as things around the room began to float. The remote, his paper, even the ottoman lifted from its spot on the floor. "Gabriel, I believe you're losing control of your powers. Let's take some deep breaths, shall we?"

He was right. She had lost all control. She squeezed her eyes shut as the sound of his thoughts pounded in her head like a TV at full volume. The downstairs neighbors' thinking about where they should go for lunch filled her brain with images of burgers, sandwiches, and fries. She was bombarded by emotions from all directions. It was impossible to tell which were hers and which were other people's. It was like she was a teenager again, the sensory overload too much for her mind to take. She shook as an argument from a couple on the street several stories below boomed in her head. She started to hyperventilate as she fell to her knees. She could feel the heat rising in her chest as her skin began to glow. Tears sprung from her eyes as she opened them, seeing the worried look on her brother's face. He was too close. As her tears evaporated from the heat, she was able to scream out a single word of warning. "RUN!" Bar stools, the sofa, and the refrigerator all floated up from the floor. Kitchen drawers flew open, sending silverware flying. A butter knife implanted itself in Lucifer's leg. He pulled it out, dropping it to the ground as the bedroom doors burst open, blankets and pillows being thrown into the hall where picture frames fell, smashing onto the hardwood. Lucifer's eyes grew wide as he saw Gabriel's hair float up. She screamed, throwing her head back as appliances and furniture crashed to the floor and her body was engulfed in flames. He flew back, shielding himself behind the island, avoiding the initial blast. She continued to scream through the plumes of smoke and fire as Lucifer peeked over the counter. When he was sure it was safe, he rushed to open the kitchen window, pulling in a gust of wind strong enough to put out the flames. It knocked her into the hall where he followed, covering her charred skin in a comforter as she healed.

"I'm sorry," she panted.

He knelt next to her, picking up a shard of glass and tossing it aside. "I've never seen you so upset. I'm by no means an expert on heartbreak, but does it really justify suicide by Holy Fire?"

"It was an accident," she grunted, standing up and going to her room where she threw on some non-burned-to-ashes clothes. She put her hand to her temple as she winced, the thoughts and feelings of others still ringing in her overworked mind. She emerged from her room, hopping on one foot as she put her boots on. She passed her brother and found her phone on the kitchen floor. The screen was only a little cracked, so she put it in her pocket and headed for the door.

"Gabriel," Lucifer called after her. She stopped to look at him. "She will come to her senses."

She nodded, having no idea if he was right, but appreciating the sincerity in his tone all the same. "I'm going out." She left, closing the door behind her harder than she intended to.

He leaned on the island and shook his head. "Well, nothing good can come from that."

Chapter 6

Michelle breathed in the late-morning air as the sun warmed her skin. The early-autumn breeze blew through her curls as she watched Will come back to the park bench, two ice cream cones in hand. He offered her one and sat, looking out at the sea of people going about their day in the park, walking dogs, playing Frisbee, and having picnics. By the time Michelle had taken two bites, he was nearly finished. She held hers out to him, still full from the massive breakfast he'd prepared for her earlier.

"Are you sure?" he asked.

"I'm not hungry."

He took it, happily eating as she smiled at him.

"I never asked, how do you like the city?"

He swallowed his last bite and put his arm around her. "Jury's still out. It's definitely different than Southport. Louder. And, there's a smell."

"Garbage mixed with cooking street food," she told him. "You get used to it."

"Hmm."

"I feel like I should tell you something."

His heart jumped as he turned to face her.

"When I was a," she glanced around before whispering, "Vampire," She cleared her throat. "I did some things."

He took a deep breath, fearing the worst. "Things? Like, with dudes?"

She scrunched her eyebrows and tilted her head. "Dudes?"

"I mean, I'll understand. I was dead, so,"

"What? No, I didn't," She looked around again. "I didn't *sleep* with anyone. I meant like, violent things. Last night, when I was on my walk, a guy was trying to kill some girl, so I," She covered her mouth, fearful of what he'd think of her once he knew the truth.

He put his hand on her knee. "You protected her?"

"Yeah," she said, covering his hand with hers. "Yeah, but,"

"But, nothing. You saw someone that needed help and you helped them. I can't fault you for that."

"There was another time, in Southport, when I was hiding from Allydia. That guy from the bowling alley tried to kidnap me off the street and I," Tears welled in her eyes. "What I did to him was--"

"I don't care."

She looked confused. "You don't care?"

"No. That guy was a monster. If you hadn't stopped me, I would have killed him myself that night. Besides, you weren't yourself. I know you'd never hurt anyone on purpose as a human."

"How can you be sure?"

He wiped away her tears. "Because you're crying just thinking about it."

She laughed and held his hand, kissing the back of it before taking a serious tone. "You know I don't blame you for the things you did before, either, right?"

"I know," His eyes darkened as he thought about the donut shop burning, the smell of his father's smoldering flesh, and the look on his grandfather's face as he died. "But, I do."

"You weren't right, Will."

"No, I wasn't. But, I thought I was. I thought I was doing the right thing, burning down the town, killing my dad. I really believed I was saving them...from me. Gabriel's girlfriend swears she fixed me, but there will always be this part of me that won't believe it. I'll never be able to trust my own judgement. Not fully."

She touched his cheek and gave him a reassuring smile. "I'll just have to keep an eye on you, then." He smiled back and kissed her, relaxing his shoulders as her lips soothed him, still hardly able to believe that he was lucky enough to be loved by someone as amazing as her.

"Allydia's not here," Navid said, stepping aside to let Gabriel in. His heart skipped a beat when he saw her, so he averted his glance, hoping not to make an ass of himself. "She's off at her bloke's."

"Don't care." She hurried past him, opening kitchen drawers and cabinets, rummaging through them before moving on to the hall closet.

"Hey, I wanted to say thanks for all the food. It was very kind of you. What are you lookin' for?" he asked as she slammed it shut.

"Where'd she put it?"

"What?"

She went to the living room, looking under couch cushions and putting her hands on her hips when it seemed her search had been fruitless. "The drugs. She used to keep all kinds, not that she ever did them. Just in case she had a guest that wanted to partake, you understand. She must have gotten rid of them before she invited you to stay because, you know," she gestured to him. "Cop."

"Detective, but fair enough."

She shut her eyes, the sound of other people's thoughts like a punch to the head.

"Are you all right?"

She squinted, the sensory overload making it hard to focus. "No."

"Do you need to go to hospital?"

She laughed. "They wouldn't know what to do with me."

"Would you like some tea? I have Chamomile, Earl Grey, Assam,"

She took a closer look at him, his feelings beginning to drown out the noise from the street and surrounding apartments. "You're worried about me."

"Well, yeah. You come in here, turnin' the place upside down hunting for drugs, obviously in some kinda pain. Anyone right in the head would be."

"You'd be surprised." She gawked at him, his genuine concern for her well-being helping to settle her mind even as it confused her.

"Now, you're the one starin'."

"Sorry, I'm just not used to people, you know, giving a shit."

"I find that hard to believe."

"I'm sorry I freaked you out, storming in here like that. My girlfriend dumped me and I kind of lost it. Maybe dumped? Not sure."

His mouth fell open. "Is she daft?"

She couldn't help but take offense. "No."

"I mean, pardon my sayin', but you're stunnin', not to mention the powerful angel bit. I don't care if she *is* a mega-powerful witch, she's lucky to have your attention. Bird must be off her trolley."

"Dude, don't flirt with me right now. I will climb you like Everest."

He was taken aback, swallowing hard as he tried not to appear nervous. "I thought you were gay."

"Pan."

"Oh." He raised his eyebrows, holding his hands in front of himself as he tried to will away his growing erection. "And, you know everything about me? How I'm feelin'?"

"Yeah."

"Well, *that's* not embarrassin'."

She eyed him like a wild animal, unsure of where his emotions ended and hers began. His desire became her own as she was overwhelmed, not by the thoughts of others, but by her sudden attraction to him. She looked down at his hands and back up at him. "You've got *nothing* to be embarrassed about."

His heart beat faster as he took a step back, his legs bumping into the sofa. "I'm trying very hard not to kiss you."

She closed the space between them, the smell of his cologne enveloping her senses. Her forehead brushed his cheek as he bit his lip. She closed her eyes. "I shouldn't let you."

"It's inappropriate, yeah?"

"Very." She looked up at him again, putting her fingertips to his chin before standing on her tiptoes and kissing him. He closed his eyes, letting his hands wander to her waist. As their kissing grew in intensity, he wrapped his arms around her, pulling her close. She tore his shirt off and pushed him down onto the couch before climbing on top of him and throwing her own shirt to the floor. "Bro, I am gonna worship that D like it's a fucking deity." She kissed him again, removing her bra and dropping it to the floor. She slid her hands over his chest, up to his neck, and back down again while he ran his over her thighs as they straddled him. "Mm," she grunted as her mind began to clear. She grabbed his face and pushed away, sighing as she debated. "Probably a bad idea, right?"

"The worst," he agreed, going in for another kiss. She held back.

"See, normally when I'm upset, I jump on the nearest dick and ride it until I calm down. But, you're not looking for a casual hook-up. You're a decent dude. I'd just be using you for your body, and you deserve better."

"I'm all right with it. Use me. Use me all day."

She laughed and stood. "Sorry, but there might still be a chance I can fix things with Wendy but there definitely won't be if I do, you know, you." She felt bad for him, sitting there all worked up with nowhere to go. She sighed. "Give me your phone."

"What for?" He took it from his pocket and handed it over.

She took a picture of herself from the neck down and tossed it back to him. "Here. For the spank bank." She put her clothes back on and left, making sure the door was locked to give him some privacy.

Navid sat alone, his heart still beating out of control, beads of sweat on his temples. "Well, that was…somethin'." He looked down at his phone and shrugged, setting it on the arm of the sofa and unzipping his pants.

Outside, Gabriel was again bombarded by noise. The thoughts of pedestrians, cab drivers, and bike messengers all flooded her brain. She needed a quiet place. She needed her brother.

While Allydia took a nap in his bedroom, Wyatt made a list of things he thought might make her more comfortable as she got re-acclimated to human life. Sunglasses, sweaters, and the ice cream she'd told him she recently discovered. He planned to surprise her with the gifts, but as he was about to leave, Gabriel burst through the door, flying into his arms and sobbing into his chest. He held her close and rubbed her back. "What happened?"

"Shh," she ordered, letting the sound of his heartbeat, strong and steady, drown out the other noises in her head. She was shaking, so he smoothed the back of her hair and kissed the top of her head.

"Okay," he whispered, resting his cheek on her head. "You're okay."

Chapter 7

The crow perched itself on top of the dilapidated cabin as Julia stepped off of Moll Dyer Road and trekked the rest of the way through the woods to meet him. Outside, the cabin looked as if it had been left to rot since 1697. The wood was grayed and crumbling. Even the grass surrounding the building had been dead so long, only a few brown and yellow blades sprung from the dry soil. She knew, though, that this was the preferred meeting place of the Dyer coven, one of the oldest and most powerful covens in the country. Leonardtown was steeped in their history and Julia hoped to enlist the sisters in her effort to take Grace's magic by force. She would offer to join them, bringing that power with her, strengthening their coven even more, making them a force to be reckoned with beyond their wildest imaginations. She went over the pitch in her head as she prepared to knock on the door, Griffin's impatient squawking distracting her from her thoughts. "Pipe down," she hissed, closing her eyes and taking a deep breath. The bird went quiet and she cracked her neck, taking one final shaky breath before rapping on the door.

An African-American woman answered, the scowl on her face making Julia's heart leap to her throat. She was tall in stature with broad shoulders and striking features. Her lumbering presence accompanied by the massive amount of power flowing from her was intimidating, to say the least. Julia felt like a child before her at five-three and a hundred and twenty pounds. She could feel her freckled cheeks blush as she nervously tried to remember her speech.

"Well, come on in, then," the woman huffed, stepping aside as she walked through and closing the door behind her. Inside was a different universe, a small palace of marble-covered floors and gold-lined walls. Eleven more women filled the room lit brightly with crystal chandeliers that seemed to glow of their own accord. *A full coven*, she thought. They wouldn't need another member. Still, she was sure they'd want her once they heard what she was offering.

"A witch," the first woman informed the others. They looked her over, some with interest, others with derision.

"Mediocre at best," a blonde in the corner assessed.

"Teleportation powers," another said. "Seems handy."

"She reeks of desperation," a middle-aged brunette dismissed.

"You've been shunned," an older woman determined, approaching her with a skeptical glare. "I can smell it all over you. Who were you with? Too weak to be a Gowdie. Too white to be a Laveau. You a Kyteler heir? I thought they stopped practicing in what, the eighteen hundreds?"

"Yes, I am and they did," she answered, painfully aware of all the eyes on her. "I was with the Tituban coven in New York."

"Grace's coven?" the older woman asked, her eyebrows raised.

She's impressed, Julia thought. *I'm in.* She nodded.

"I heard about your Priestess. My condolences."

"Thank you. That's why I'm here."

"Is it? Because from where I'm standing, it looks like you're here to find a new coven to take you in."

"Well, yes, ma'am, but I don't come empty-handed. Grace hid her magic from the rest of us. I tracked it to an apartment in Tribeca where it had been claimed by an outsider."

"That's not possible," the woman argued. "The only way someone from outside the coven would have access to a fallen Priestesses' magic would be if..." She stepped back. "*A blood relative?*"

Julia nodded. "I'm offering to join our covens, once I take Grace's over. I have a bit of the witch's blood. I can use it to track her and siphon the magic from--"

"Are you out of your mind?!" she laughed, the other women in the room looking shocked as they, too, held back nervous laughter. "If there's a blood-born Tiutuban witch carrying Grace's magic on top of her own, you should run and hide, not plot war with your coven."

She clenched her jaw, speaking as calmly as she could through gritted teeth. "Grace's magic belongs to the coven. If they won't take me back, her power will be *mine*. I need allies."

"Girl, what you need is a psych evaluation. I knew Grace. We tussled back in the day. The amount of power she wielded would crush you under its weight. *If* you *somehow* shook it free of the Ttuban witch, it would *boil you alive*. I would advise you to forget about this, but you seem set, so I'll ask you to take your leave...and don't come back."

She held her hand out as if to say 'stop', sending Julia sliding back to the reopened door and out onto the porch. The door slammed in front of her, dashing her hopes as she heard the clacking of three locks latching. From the roof, the crow squawked and flapped its wings.

She turned and stomped back toward the road. "Shut up, Griffin."

Every witch in North America worth her salt knew the story of Isobel Gowdie. After a torture-forced confession in Auldearn, she'd tricked her executioners into hanging and burning the long-dead body of a local child in her place. The boy had died of fever, his corpse buried on the outskirts of Nairn for fear of contamination. It had been easy to dig him up and apply the glamour. Once everyone was convinced she was dead, Isobel fled to The New World where she used maleficium to coerce the founder of Providence to grant her asylum. By the next summer, she'd formed a new coven, using blood magic to spread her power evenly to all members. With her DNA now part of them, they had children who would carry the magic, as well. Now, more than three hundred and fifty years later, the Gowdie coven was made up strictly of the descendants of Isobel's original coven. Outsiders were forbidden from setting foot on their property, a towering three-story, seven-bedroom Italianate in College Hill with a four-car garage and guest house. Witches from all over the world knew to stay away from the Cushing Street mansion for fear of being executed on sight. The Gowdies were solitary, ruthless, and played by their own set of rules. They were the only one of the original covens that allowed male members. The rest had outlawed them when a group of male witches formed a secret society in 1854 whose sole purpose was to annex several territories as slave states and rule over all non-witches in those places, using the forced labor of the "ungifted" to amass fortunes for their members. Men were deemed too power-hungry and self-serving to handle magic, so from then on, when a male witch was born, his powers were stripped. The Gowdies deemed the practice unnecessary and cruel and refused to partake in what they saw as a criminal act. Their male witches were as much a part of their coven as the women, with the same rights and responsibilities as the rest. They'd even had male leaders over the years, the last Priest having died by suicide in October of 1987 when he'd lost his personal fortune in the stock market crash. Now, his daughter, Blair was High Priestess. In her late forties and as beautiful as ever, Blair ran the coven like a machine. Half the members were related to her in one way or another and the other half were either in love with her or terrified of her. She slinked around the mansion imposing her will on the others with minimal effort, none of them daring to oppose her under any circumstances. They weren't victims, however, each of them as sinister as she, taking joy in the pain they inflicted on their victims. They used any sort of dark magic necessary to accomplish their goals, which were generally money-based and indulgent. They compelled bank tellers to rob their employers' vaults and leave the sacks of cash at their doorstep. They glamoured themselves to appear as the spouses of politicians, only revealing their true faces once in the act of adultery, having secret cameras taking incriminating pictures for the purpose of blackmailing them later. When one of them would get sick, whether it be a cold or cancer, they'd transfer their ailment to someone in town that had annoyed them in some way. As far as witches went, the Gowdies were as devious and heartless as they came.

 Now, standing just a few feet from their door, Julia was wondering if she'd made a mistake in coming to them. Even Griffin refused to land on anything closer than a tree across the street. She stood under its branches and thought it over. If they agreed to help her siphon Grace's magic, they'd no doubt want a piece of it for themselves. On the other hand, without them, she was alone and she was in no way strong enough to go against this Wendy on her own. She *could* try the Leveaus in New Orleans, but they were sure to send her away, the kind of magic they practiced requiring a delicate balance of light and dark. They'd see what she was trying to do as selfish and may even bind her powers as a precaution against upsetting the natural order of things. If she pissed off the Gowdies, though, she could end up dead.

Before she'd made a decision, she found herself inside the giant house, surrounded by well-dressed witches of varying ages. There were several redheads and blondes with similar features; siblings, she assumed. The rest were of varying ethnicities, all sharing the same bothered expression as they sized her up. She immediately recognized Blair. Her beauty was notorious. Her full lips and bright eyes were the envy of insecure witches all over the East, though rumors spread that it was all a show, a glamour to cover her true face. That could have been jealousy, of course, but no one would ever know with how secretive the Gowdie coven was.

The Priestess folded her slender arms and tapped her glossy red nails on her porcelain skin as she looked her over. "Tituban," she mused. "How is your coven still functioning without Grace? She was the only one of you with any real power."

"You're telling me," she croaked, unnerved by the way they'd blinked her into the house.

"The Dyers called, said you were hell-bent on doing something foolish. You've come seeking assistance?"

She nodded. The group looked amused.

"She's cute," one of the blonde men said. "Can I keep her?"

"Do you mind sharing, cousin?" another man asked.

"Not at all."

"Just let me play with her a little first," an Asian woman sneered.

"I'll get the video camera."

"She won't be staying," Blair told them, ignoring the disappointed looks on their faces. She waved at them to stand behind her, ensuring she couldn't flee. They followed orders as she shifted her weight from one foot to another and bit the inside of her cheek. "You want us to what, distract the witch while you take her power for yourself?"

She swallowed hard. "Basically."

"And in return for our help, you'll join us, enriching our coven?"

"Well,"

"And, we should agree? We should bend to your will? You, a shunned witch lacking in discipline or decorum, holding less magic in her entire body than I do in my big toe?" The others snickered. "Honestly, I can't decide if I should admire your conviction or pity you for your obvious lack of intellect."

She fumed, her cheeks burning hot as she clenched her fists at her sides.

Blair tossed her strawberry blonde locks off her shoulder and shook her head. "What you offer is insufficient. We don't work for others and we don't take in a lesser coven's rejects. Pure Tituban magic, though, *that's* of interest. So I have a counter. You give me what I need to find this Tituban witch and I won't carve out your entrails and use them in my next divination."

She stared daggers at the Priestess, her anger boiling over.

"You won't talk? That's fine. I don't need you to." She grabbed the sides of Julia's head, her eyes boring into hers, her face turning red. "Zeige mir."

Julia began to convulse as Blair searched her mind, the images of memories flashing in her minds-eye like movie clips. She saw the name 'Wendy' on the letter in the New York apartment. She saw the girl, Poe, tangled up and tortured. She saw the name of the town where Grace's coven resided and she saw the address of the house Julia thought would be the most likely place Wendy would be hiding. Blair let go, leaving Julia to fall in a heap on the dark hardwood. "Tarrytown," she smirked, looking back at the others. "Packs some snacks. We're going on a road trip."

Suddenly, Julia was back out on the sidewalk across the street, fetal on the ground under the tree where the crow still perched. She held a hand to her head as she got to her feet. Dizzy and unwanting of any further attention from the Gowdies, she teleported herself back to her house in Tarrytown.

A block away from the mansion, a man slumped in the driver's seat of a rusted-out pickup, cell phone in hand, its camera pointed at the bird that now took flight. He looked back to the house as he sent the video to his boss and pulled up his number. He hit 'call' and put the phone to his ear.

"Something's up," he told the person on the other end, picking up his binoculars and looking through them into the front window of the coven's sanctuary. He could see them in what looked like an important conversation, their leader grinning from ear to ear. "I'll keep you posted."

She sat at her kitchen table, head in hands, tears of frustration pooling in her eyes. She had to get to Wendy before the Gowdies. If they got hold of Grace's magic, that was it. She'd be without a coven and without any real power forever. She couldn't let it happen. She went to a drawer and pulled out the book she'd swiped from Grace's house the last time she was there. There had to be something useful in it. *Something* to help her take back what was rightfully hers.

After a few minutes of flipping through pages of family anecdotes and herbal remedies, she came upon a page written in a different ink. It was faded, clearly older than the other pages, and had a peculiar energy about it as if the paper itself served as a warning. Written in Latin, it described the events of a spell gone wrong in old Salem. A young girl had inadvertently summoned a creature of some kind, a strange man referring to it as 'Moloch'. The girl had promised it something in return for the power to bring the dead back to life. The creature had agreed, but Tituba put an end to it, capturing the monster in a statue with seven locks and burying it in one of her hiding places.

She slammed the book shut and sat back in her chair, arms crossed and brow furrowed. She knew Tituba's woods well. Grace had taken the coven there several times over the years for special occasions: the birth of a new witch, May Eve, Litha, and even a few weddings were performed there, the witches eager to have their unions blessed by Tituba's spirit. Julia was sure she would have no problem finding the statue if that's what she decided to do. Unlocking it may be trickier, but she could figure it out. It was risky, though. She knew by the vibes coming from the page that this creature was mischievous if not altogether dark. What would it want in return for its help? Would it even do as she asked? She'd have to consider it carefully, given that the ramifications were unknown. She'd have to hurry, though. The Gowdies were on their way.

Chapter 8

Hartley stood on the doorstep of the brick railroad-style apartment on 73rd Street in Queens, the sound of a dog barking a few doors down startling her as she took in her surroundings. It had been more than fifty years since she'd been here but it looked exactly the same. Same geometric pattern in the front window, same peaked porch roof above the door. Even the patch of dirt that acted as her front yard that she'd spend hours a day playing in as a child remained identical, not a speck of green in sight. She wasn't entirely sure what she was doing there, except that she felt she needed to come. Allydia had told her to live her life as she saw fit, that she was free. She didn't feel that way, though. For decades, she avoided this place, the memories too upsetting to relive. It haunted her like the screams of the Wailing Woman from the ghost story her mother had told her all those years ago. Now, standing in front of her childhood home, Hartley felt more afraid than she had when she'd first heard the tale as a five-year-old. She took a breath and tightened her ponytail, jumping from one foot to the other, and closing her eyes. "Let's go, bitch," she muttered to herself. She knocked on the door and stood still, opening her eyes as a woman in pink scrubs answered. She looked to be in her early fifties, heavy set with high cheekbones and dull eyes. Definitely *not* her mother.

"Can I help you?" the nurse asked politely.

She was flustered but quickly regained her composure. "I'm sorry, I was looking for Gloria Morales."

The woman's face lit up. "Oh, of course, come in!" She let her in and closed the door, locking the deadbolt as Hartley glanced around the room. It was exactly the same, from the herringbone pattern on the floor to the plastic on the sofa. A portrait of white Jesus still hung on the living room wall and crosses adorned the tops of every door frame. Growing up here had felt so oppressive and foreboding. Now, though, as she took in the familiar scent of lemon furniture polish, it seemed smaller somehow. It was just a building. It had no power over her.

"Gloria doesn't get many visitors these days, aside from Father Daniel, of course," the woman said. "He comes a few times a week. How do you know her?"

As she looked around, it occurred to her that her mother still hadn't made an appearance. Who was this woman and why was she there? "I'm her...granddaughter."

"Oh! I'm sorry, I'm just surprised. She's never mentioned you. I'm sure you're anxious to see her. She's right through there." She pointed to the door of her parents' bedroom. "I'll leave you two alone, let you catch up. It's my lunch break, anyway. She shouldn't need anything. She's been relatively comfortable the last few days. I'll be back in about an hour." The woman left, locking the door back from the outside.

Hartley felt her heart begin to race as she approached the bedroom door. Her mother was ninety-one and from what she'd discerned, not in the best of health. Her stomach twisted at the thought of what she might find on the other side of the door as she turned the knob. What would she say? Why was she even there?

"Wanda?" the old woman asked, her voice soft. She tried to lift her head to get a look at the woman entering her room but was too weak, tired from the heavy doses of medication she was on. She was lying in a hospital bed, the top half raised slightly. She looked frail, not like the tough-as-nails mother she'd been raised by.

"No, Gloria," she said, stepping closer. "My name's Hartley. Your son, Hart, was my father."

"Hart?" She squinted with cloudy eyes to see her face.

Hartley sat in the chair next to the bed. "Yes, ma'am. I'm your granddaughter."

Gloria's expression went from confused to joyful. "Hart! My baby! I'm so happy to see you!" She took her face in her hands and kissed both cheeks.

"No, ma'am," she lied. "I'm *Hartley*, your--"

She laughed. "Las tonterias. My vision may be going along with the rest of me, but I would recognize my sweet boy anywhere. How could I not know who you are? You are my soul. My heart. Where did you think your name came from, mm? How are you, Papi?"

She didn't know what to say. Being called by her deadname didn't bother her as much as the fact that her mother seemed to have forgotten how horribly she'd let her father treat her back in the day. The beatings when he'd find her wearing her mother's makeup. The lectures about morality. The slurs. The "therapy". She had no idea how with it her mother was, what medicine she was taking, or even what disease she had. She didn't know if she knew what she was saying or if she was too doped up to know right from left, but this was her shot. This was her chance to get it all off her chest. The abuse, the torture, the pain. She'd hear it all. She'd be made to remember it the way Hartley had for all those years. She'd tell her how cruel they'd been. How ignorant and self-righteous. She'd tell her how miserable she'd been growing up in that household of zealots and how happy she'd been since coming out as trans. She'd spill her truth on her like candy from a pinata and leave before she had the chance to respond. It was time. This was her opportunity. But, as she sat there, looking into her mother's milky eyes, knowing this may be the last time she'd ever see her alive, she couldn't do it. No matter what she'd done, no matter what she'd let her father do, she was still her mother and she couldn't bear to break her heart.

 Tears slid down her rouged cheeks and she lowered her head as she held her mother's hand. "I'm fine, Mami."

 "Why are you crying, my angel? Are you worried about your father? Because he can't hurt you anymore."

 She lifted her eyes to look at her again. "What do you mean?"

 "It took a few weeks," Gloria said, her voice getting fainter. "Just a pinch every night. Not enough that he could taste it. Every dinner for three weeks."

 Her eyes grew to saucers, remembering her father's obituary in the paper twenty or so years before. All it had said about how he'd died was that it had been 'natural causes'. He was in his late sixties by then, so she hadn't questioned it. The truth was, she hadn't much cared. The man was horrible and deserved whatever heart attack or stroke that had taken him. But, this? "What are you saying, Mami?"

 "He was a proud man, your father. Would never admit when he was wrong. But, I could tell, he knew. He knew what he did to you was a sin. Kicking you out, disowning you like that. I begged him to bring you home. For thirty years, I begged him. But, he was stubborn. After that final dinner, his favorite, Sopa De Lima, my begging came to an end." Her eyes fluttered closed and her breathing slowed.

Hartley covered her mouth, shocked by what she was hearing.

"I was so happy that...the last thing I saw in his eyes...was regret." She began to quietly snore as Hartley wiped the tears from her face with trembling hands.

"Holy shit," she whispered. All this time, she thought she'd been so willing to commit acts of torture and kill people with no real remorse because she'd been a vampire. Turns out, it was genetic.

Back at her apartment, Hartley cuddled with her cat on the couch, taking refuge from the day and its unrelenting sunshine. Marilyn seemed unfazed by the change in her owner, purring happily on her lap as she always did. Vampire or human, it made no difference to her. "As long as I keep you in food and catnip, you're a content kitty, huh?" Hartley said, petting her back as she drifted off for a nap. A knock came on the door, startling the cat who jumped up and found a new place to sleep in the corner of the sofa. Hartley got up and answered it, surprised to see Oliver standing on the other side. "I thought you went back to Atlantic City," she said, letting him in and closing the door behind him.

"I was going to but," He put his hands on his hips, his pained expression causing her to tilt her head like a confused dog. He grunted and took her hands in his. "Come with me."

"What?"

"Live with me."

"You're crazy."

"I'm serious. Aside from the genocide, nearly getting burned alive, and the sudden change in species, being with you again has been incredible."

She laughed. "I think you need to eat something."

"I need *you*, Hartley. Come on. What else have you got to do today? Just try it. Give it a week. If you hate it, you can always leave me...shattered in a million pieces and contemplating celibacy as a lifestyle choice."

She laughed again and folded her arms, his charming accent giving her butterflies. "I'd have to bring Marilyn."

"A threesome? I didn't think you liked to share but if that's what you want--"

"My cat," she tittered, glancing over to the couch and back at him.

He looked at the ball of fur curled up in the corner and laughed. "Oh! Yeah, sure. Bring the cat. Get a dog. We can have an entire menagerie if you like. What do ya say?"

She chewed on her bottom lip and squinted at him, shaking her head and giving him a sly smile. "All right, we can *try it* but only because you look extra cute in that shirt. Green was always your color."

"Yes!" He scooped her up and swung her around as she giggled, forgetting for a moment about her mother's confession and how pitiful she looked lying in the hospital bed. Now, she just felt happy and she wanted to stay in that bliss for as long as she could.

Chapter 9

"So, your girlfriend's an angel? Lucifer's real?" Poe asked as they entered the house in Tarrytown.

"Yeah," Wendy told her.

"I think my head's gonna explode."

"Don't tell anyone. I'm pretty sure it would be like, Apocalyptically bad if word got out. And, I'm not sure she's my girlfriend anymore."

She scoffed as she put Wendy's bags on the bed in Grace's old room. "You'll forgive her. She was just looking out for you."

"I guess. Who's this?" She bent down and smiled, petting the rabbit that hopped into the room to greet them.

"That's Raven."

"Your familiar?"

She nodded, passing by and walking to the kitchen where she got a fresh bowl of greens together for the bunny's lunch.

Wendy followed, sitting at the table as Poe dropped into a chair, resting her chin on her fist. "Thanks for letting me crash here."

"No problem. So, you don't have a familiar?"

"No," Wendy said. "What I do can get pretty dangerous and I always thought it'd be better to go it alone. Didn't want anyone else to get hurt if I messed something up."

"Oh," she said, raising a knowing eyebrow.

"What?"

"You're not used to anyone caring about you."

"So?"

"So, when your girl tried to protect you, it freaked you out."

"It didn't *freak me out*. It pissed me off."

"Did it *really*, or was it just a good excuse to end things before she could get hurt by some witchy bullshit?"

She folded her hands. "I'm pretty sure God's Messenger can't be taken down by a rogue witch with a hard-on for my magic."

"I'm not talking about Julia, specifically. And, maybe she can't be hurt by her, or *anything*. But, your subconscious doesn't know that."

She pursed her lips and let out an exasperated sigh. "You're making some good points, Poe. Gotta say...it's kind of obnoxious."

A crash came from the living room, jolting them from their seats. "Julia," Poe whispered.

"Doubt it," Wendy said, feeling the immense power coming from the front door. "Feels like..." They went to the living room where a group of twelve witches stood, all wearing the same smug grin. "Gowdies."

"Which one of you is the Tituban witch?" a woman in a flowing red dress asked, stepping toward them.

"Blair, right?" Wendy said, giving her a once-over. "The rumors are true, then. You're smokin'."

"Flattery," Blair chirped. "Unexpected, but it won't distract me. I've come for Grace's magic. Hand it over willingly and I won't butcher the child."

"I'm not a child," Poe snapped.

"Shh." Wendy held her arm out to keep her a few steps behind her, keeping her eyes on the Priestess. "How did you find me?"

Blair rolled her eyes. "Ugh, that imbecile from Grace's coven tried to acquire my services in taking your power for herself. She apparently didn't know what she was walking into."

"I won't give you my power. If it didn't kill you, it would make you even more power-hungry and megalomaniacal than you already are."

She laughed. "Dear girl, how naive do you think I am? Grace's magic is powerful beyond measure. I wouldn't dare take it all into myself. I'm not suicidal."

Wendy wrinkled her brow.

"No, no. I will share the power with my family. That magic would incinerate just one of us, but divide it by twelve..." She held her hands out and flicked her fingers causing the room to shake. After a few seconds, the whole house was rattling.

"Sturm!" a redhead shouted. Thunder clapped above them so loud, it sounded like it was coming from inside the house. A man opened his mouth, sucking in a deep breath and blowing it out, filling the room with a gust of wind so strong, it knocked Poe to the floor.

"It's real cute," Wendy called over the noise. "But, it won't affect me."

Blair scrunched her nose. "Ubertragen!"

"Is that German?"

She held her hand out in front of her as if asking for money. "UBERTRAGEN!"

"I'm gonna have to look that up, hold on!" Wendy took her phone from her pocket and typed the word into a translator app. "Oh! 'Transfer'! That won't work on me!"

The house quaked more, flinging pictures from the walls as Blair's face turned a deep shade of red.

"Hey, you match your dress!"

"Gib es vorbei!"

"It won't work!" she yelled again, hardly able to hear her own voice over the interior thunderstorm. "I can't...I can't be...UGH! Quiescis!" The room went still. "Much better," she said, grateful for the quiet. "Like I was trying to tell you, I can't be spelled."

"Of course you can!" Blair defied. "Ubertragen!"

She sighed. "No, really, I can't. Ancient magic. I'm warded from any supernatural harm. You guys aren't, though. Supernatet."

All twelve Gowdie witches lifted from the ground, hovering in midair, the horror on their faces causing Poe to giggle.

Wendy clasped her hands in front of her as she walked around the room, stepping between the floating witches and shaking her head. "You Gowdies, man. You're all terrorism and greed. Did you not get enough hugs as kids, or what?"

"Lass mich gehen!" the mouth-breather griped.

"Is that another spell, or are you just bitching?"

"Fine!" Blair relented, annoyance and dread in her voice. "We'll go. We won't come for you again."

"See, I wish I could believe you."

"What are you gonna do with them?" Poe asked.

"What someone should've done a long time ago." She went to the bedroom and opened one of the suitcases. "I knew this would come in handy one of these days." She held up an instant camera and took a photo of the group.

Blair's face fell, going stark white as her eyes widened. "What are you doing?"

Wendy shook the picture as it developed and walked back to stand next to Poe. "Got any ribbon?"

"Sure," she said, scurrying to the kitchen and fetching a spool of black ribbon from a drawer. She handed it to Wendy.

"Don't!" Blair begged.

Wendy ignored her, wrapping the photo with the ribbon until the entire image was covered. "Scissors?"

"Oh, right." Poe rushed back to retrieve a pair of orange-handled sewing scissors and brought them back. Wendy snipped the ribbon and handed the spool and scissors to Poe, tucking the end in so nothing was left loose.

"You wouldn't dare!" Blair shouted. The others squirmed, unable to break free from Wendy's floating prison.

"You brought this on yourself," she told her, taking the picture in both hands. She cleared her throat. "Sunt vinctum ex usura magicae aeternum."

The group screamed, sweat dripping from their foreheads as they realized what had been done to them.

"NO!" Blair bellowed.

"It had to be done," Wendy said. "You people have given magic a bad name for centuries. I don't know why no one bound your powers before now."

"No one's been strong enough," Poe explained. "Grace wanted to. She told me she tried a few times years ago, but it never worked. Damn, you're like, Super Witch."

She snickered. "Maybe I'll get tee-shirts made."

"You'll pay for this!" Blair warned. "We'll get our powers back and we'll--"

She rolled her eyes. "Relinquo." They disappeared, sent back to their house in Providence with a single word. "Well, that was exciting. Let's go bury this and get some lunch. I'm starving."

Poe nodded, following her through the kitchen and out the back door, Raven hopping along behind them.

The early afternoon sun all but disappeared behind the leaves of the massive oak trees as Julia headed deep into the forest. Sparse rays peppered the landscape, providing just enough light to lead her to the clearing where Tituba used to perform her most sacred rituals. "Ostendeo," she demanded. The ground opened before her, centuries of earth and rock making way for the perfectly preserved tree stump to rise up, its secrets no longer hidden. She reached inside, pulling out candles and bundles of dried herbs. Finally, she found what she'd been looking for, the small bronze statue that held the key to all of her ambitions. It was hideous, its face that of a cow's twisted in anguish. Its body resembled a naked man's, the hands stretched out as if in offering. "Seven locks," she muttered, looking it over, the seams of the chambers barely visible. She cracked her neck and began. "Laxo." One chamber burst open from the statue's right leg. "Revelabit." Four more sprung open from its back. "Recludo." A tiny chamber emerged from the top of the figure's head. She blew out an uneasy breath as she prepared to give the last command. She closed her eyes and gripped the figure tight, as if it would slip away before she could finish the spell, ruining her plans. She leaned against a tree and opened her eyes. "Dabit fructum." She heard a sharp click inside the figure as sulfuric smoke seeped from its openings. She coughed, waving the black fog away, still holding tight to the idol. The dark cloud wafted a few feet away, slowly forming an opaque shadow in the shape of a faceless man. She swallowed the bile that came up in her throat as the smell grew stronger and the shadow moved closer.

"Why have you freed me, witch?" the creature hissed, its voice low and snarling.

She trembled against the tree, squeezing her fingers so tightly around one of the open chambers of the figure that she drew blood. "I seek assistance."

It lurched its neck and slithered to only a few inches from her face. "You are stronger than the last girl that summoned me to this place. She had no real power. But, *you*," It was so close, it was almost touching her. "You could be of use."

"I need more power," she told it. "There's a witch that took--"

"I care nothing for your reasons. If power is what you desire, power is what I shall provide. But, nothing comes without a price."

"W-What do you want?"

"A child. One young, preferably still suckling. Bring one to me, and I will give you what you want."

"I can't do that," she said, her heart sinking as it backed away and turned its back to her. She walked toward it, her stomach aching with disappointment. "Please. I can't kidnap a baby. It's too terrible. There must be something else. Blood? I'll open a vein right now. You want to be worshiped? Here." She dropped to her knees. "I'll praise you, sing songs of your awesome power. Anything. Just tell me what to do."

It turned, putting a hand to its chin. It circled her, the leaves on the ground not making a sound as he stepped on them. "Get to your feet."

She did as she was told.

"There is something else I will have." It stood before her, hands on hips.

"Name it."

It dipped its head. "Take off your clothes."

She drew in a sharp breath. "Take off..."

"Remove your clothing and lay yourself down. Give yourself to me of your own free will and I will grant your request."

Her mind raced as she tried to quickly make a decision, but she couldn't think straight. Between the nausea from the stench and the panic over her last chance of getting what she wanted slipping through her fingers, it felt to her like there was only one option. She kicked off her shoes and pulled her top off over her head. She shimmied out of her jeans and unhooked her bra, slipping it off and dropping it to the ground. Finally, she slid off her panties and got down on her knees before lying back on the soft grass. She kept her eyes fixed on the creature as it came down on top of her, seeming to have no weight, though she could feel it on her skin, its touch slimy as if it was covered in a layer of mucus. It spread her legs wide, a strange growl emanating from its throat. It held her hands above her head as she felt it enter her, filling her completely with its slippery phallus. She closed her eyes, biting her lip as it thrust into her over and over again. As sick as she felt and as terrified as she was, her body couldn't help but react, her back arching and her hips rocking beneath the shadow's greasy touch. She groaned in pleasure, indifferent to the crow in the tree above, screeching, and flapping its wings so hard that feathers loosened and fell in a halo around her head. It flew off, the stench of sulfur making it, too feel sick.

Chapter 10

"You ready?" Will asked. Michelle squeezed his hand, her face beaming as they waited on the porch of Malik and Valerie's Connecticut home.

"I think so," she said, pressing the doorbell, hopping a little in anticipation.

"Will!" Valerie said, opening the door and giving her nephew a hug. "Come in, Sinclair's waiting for you." She let them in and closed the door. "You must be Michelle. I hear you're human again. Good for you. Vampires always gave me the heebies."

"Yes, ma'am. Me, too."

"Did you just," Valerie rolled her eyes. "What is with you two and this 'ma'am' shit?"

"Oh, I'm sorry, um,"

"Valerie."

"Right. Valerie. I was just trying to be polite."

"I know, I know," she sighed as she led them to the living room.

"Mommy!" Sinclair squealed, racing to meet them, wrapping her arms around Michelle's waist. "I'm so glad you came!"

"I'll give you all some privacy," Valerie said, patting Will on the shoulder before retreating to another room.

"Did you like my picture?" the child asked, pulling away.

"Yeah, baby," Michelle told her, fighting back tears. "It was really good."

"Hey, sweetie," Will said.

"Hi, Daddy. My other dad's waiting for you in the kitchen. He wants to make sure you're not dangerous anymore. I told him you were fine now, but he doesn't think I know what I'm talking about. Spoiler alert, I do."

He laughed. "Okay, I'll go talk to him. Be right back." He went to the kitchen, leaving mother and daughter alone for the first time in what seemed like forever.

Michelle knelt down to get a better look at Sinclair's face, seeing so much of herself there. She was the perfect combination of her and Will. She had her nose, mouth, and chin, and Will's cheeks and eyes. She had long, flowing curls held back with colorful barrettes and dimples that made Michelle's heart melt. She couldn't believe how fast she'd grown. She looked to be six or seven and spoke like a twelve-year-old. Michelle rubbed the girl's arms and smiled. "I missed you."

"I missed you, too. I'm really glad you're back. I have so much to show you! Come on!" She took her hand and led her back to the entry and up the staircase. "Did Daddy tell you about my chalkboard wall?"

In the kitchen, the men stared awkwardly at one another on opposite sides of the island. Will scratched his head then folded his hands in front of him while Malik remained still, arms folded, a skeptical scowl on his face. The silence lasted too long. Will decided he needed to break the ice. "So, Sinclair said you think I'm still psycho."

He pursed his lips, widening his eyes in surprise.

"I'm okay now. A witch did a spell. It's all under control."

"Val told me."

"But, you aren't sure."

"I'm not sure of much these days. Demons, vampires, witches. All seem like things to avoid. Magic spells. Too good to be true, if you ask me."

"That's valid. I do feel a lot better, though. And, I swear, I would never do anything to hurt Sinclair. You have to know that."

"Oh, I believe you. How long's that gonna last is the question."

Will cleared his throat, fiddling with his fingers as the room grew quiet again. "So, Malik, what do you do?"

"I'm a chef."

"Really? I got a degree in Culinary Arts. Online, but still. Where do you cook?"

"I'm a private chef and I teach classes here and there."

"Do you like it?"

"Love it."

"Can I ask you a question?"

He shrugged.

"Why don't you cook in a restaurant? You're an hour away from the food capital of the world. I'd think you'd want to be more a part of it."

"I like what I do. I don't have anyone telling me what to do. I'm my own boss. That's what's important to me."

"So, why not open your own restaurant?"

Malik chuckled. "Well, that's a nice thought, kid, but it's kind of a pipe dream. Sixty percent of new restaurants close in the first year, eighty by year five. You need a prime location to have a chance at all, and those are tens of thousands a month in rent alone. A food truck, maybe, one day. That's the smarter play."

Will leaned in, his expression quizzical. "You teaching my daughter to think that small?"

"Hey," Michelle said, entering the room and placing a hand on her boyfriend's shoulder. "Time to go. Sinclair said she needs a nap."

Malik looked at the clock on the stove. "Yep, it's about that time. I'll show you out." He got up and ushered the young couple to the front door. "See you again soon." He closed the door abruptly as Michelle cast Will a confused side-eye.

"What was that about?"

He shrugged.

They walked back to the car, stopping to give the house a final look. She sighed.

He opened the door for her. "What's wrong?"

"I didn't want to go," she admitted. "She's so awesome, Will. I love her so much."

"I know. Me, too."

She stared up at her daughter's bedroom window, tears forming in her eyes as she made the determination. "I want her back."

"Thanks for letting me hang out," Gabriel said, watching as Wyatt got her another soda from the fridge. He set it on the island in front of her and sat down, opening a can for himself and taking a sip.

"You're always welcome here, you know that."

"Yeah. I thought I'd be intruding on your time with Dia. I didn't know she'd be asleep for hours."

"She's not exactly used to her new sleep schedule."

She giggled. "No, I guess not."

"So, you ready to talk about what happened? Maybe start with why you smell like charcoal?"

"Your damn firefighter instincts," she said, taking a drink before putting the can down. "I set myself on fire a little earlier. Not a little. A lot. Lucifer had to gale-force wind me onto my ass to put me out."

He raised an eyebrow.

"It was an accident. You're not the only one that can lose control of their powers in an emotional fit. Pretty sure I broke my oven, too, not that it matters."

"Why were you upset?"

"Fight with Wendy."

"Ah."

"We might have broken up. She was super pissed."

"What'd you do?"

"I didn't tell her one of her witch friends was in trouble and now some other witch chick is salty about Wendy having her dead aunt's magic instead of her. I don't know, it seemed pretty petty to me."

"Why didn't you tell her?"

"The same reason you wouldn't have told her if you were me. I was protecting her. Those crazy bitches are out there killing each other trying to steal *her* magic. I don't know if she's a match for them. From what I saw in her friend's head, they're all pretty badass. I just watched Cam die like, twenty minutes before that girl showed up. I couldn't risk losing Wendy, too. Now, I may have, anyway."

"I'm sorry."

She shrugged, taking another sip of soda.

He stood and picked his keys up from the counter. "All right, well, I have to go." He scribbled a note telling Allydia he'd be back in a few hours. "Stay as long as you want, just lock up when you leave. Talk more later?"

"Actually, can I come with you?"

"To therapy?"

"Yeah. You don't have anything important to talk about and I could use some advice."

He laughed. "Okay, sure. It's not like it'll be the first time you've taken over one of my sessions."

Chapter 11

Allydia found the note on the counter and clicked her nails on the cool stone. She noticed two soda cans on the island, one of them marked by a smear of pale pink lipgloss. She felt a twinge of jealousy rise in her chest until she realized she'd seen that shade before. "Gabriel." She relaxed her shoulders and took a sip from the can she assumed belonged to Wyatt. The bubbles tickled her tongue and burned her throat as she swallowed the intensely sweet liquid. She set the can back in its spot and cleared her throat. "They drink this on purpose?"

A thunderous banging came from the door. Allydia's spine straightened as she was keenly aware of how much weaker she was than she used to be. Who would be pounding so hard on Wyatt's door and what would she do if they were dangerous? She thought back to what she'd told Hartley about self-defense. She'd also been trained by various senseis over thousands of years. She may not have superior strength and speed anymore, but she was far from helpless.

She went to the door and opened it, taking a step back in surprise when she saw who was standing on the other side. "Phindi, what are you--" But she was cut off before she could finish the question, taking a hard jab to the chin. "Ow!" she yelped.

"How could you do this to me?" the woman barked. "To all of us?" She went to hit her again, but Allydia blocked her punches, one after another as the former general pushed her way inside. "You betrayed us! The traitor was right. It was *you* who lost your way."

"It wasn't meant to affect the rest of you," she told her, jumping back to avoid a kick to the abdomen. "I only wanted a chance at freedom. I thought you would carry on as you were without me."

"Carry on without you?" she exploded. "*There is no us without you!* You were the dam that held back the raging sea. You were the mother of our kind. I served you faithfully for generations. I loved you!" She picked up a barstool and smashed it against the counter, shattering it against the stone. She took a broken leg and spun it in her hand as she edged closer, Allydia backing away.

"I'm sorry, Phindi. You were an excellent soldier. I care for you, truly. But, the burden of what I'd become was too great. I'd nearly forgotten who I was. And, when it cost me the man I love, I--"

"You chose *him*!" she shouted. "You chose *him* over your people! A *human*!" She charged, her makeshift stake raised. "Perhaps, after I kill you I'll wait for him to return and slaughter him, as well!"

"Hey!"

Phindi turned to the male voice calling from behind and was immediately thrown to the ground by a ball of electricity. She was stunned, but not badly hurt, the lightning of a fairly low voltage. She tried to get up, but the man stepped into the apartment, hand out, ready to fire again if she made a move. She clenched her jaw. "Another lightning wielder?"

"Thank you, Will," Allydia said as Michelle closed the door behind them. She stood between the couple and her attacker, kneeling and brushing Phindi's cheek. "I'm sorry, Duchess. Hurting you was not my intention."

Tears streamed down her face, her chest heaving as she fell apart. "What do I do now? I have nothing. *What am I* if not a warrior for the queen?"

Will chimed in, "You could go into private security."

The former vampires gave him condescending glares.

"What? It's not a ridiculous idea. I hear Cardinal Rain's looking for new management."

Dr. Stratford shifted in his seat, made visibly uncomfortable by Gabriel's presence. He turned his glance to Wyatt who sat next to her, his elbow resting on the arm of the couch, his legs crossed, ankle over knee. "Your sister?" the doctor verified.

He nodded. "Yeah. We have the same dad."

Gabriel erupted in laughter while Wyatt stifled a snicker.

"That's amusing to you?" the doctor wondered.

"It's funny because it's true."

"All right," He took off his glasses and set them on the table next to him. "So, Mr. Sinclair, why have you brought your sister to your session? Are you having trouble navigating your new-found family dynamics? Are there unresolved feelings surrounding her discovering you? Any resentments? Jealousy?"

"No."

"I'm kind of hijacking his session," she told him. "He was just gonna talk about how his girlfriend made a huge sacrifice to get him back and he feels guilty about that, blah, blah, blah. I told him on the way here she'd been thinking about it for a while. His dumping her was just the straw that broke the camel's back. He's got no reason to feel bad. Guilt-ridden is kind of his default setting, though, so."

He shot her an annoyed glance.

"What? That is accurate."

"I'm sorry, young lady," the doctor said. "But, I'm retiring soon and no longer taking new patients. Unless this is a joint session to discuss--"

She took a wad of hundred dollar bills from her back pocket and threw it on the coffee table. The doctor looked at it and back to her before putting his glasses back on and picking up a notebook and pen. "What do you want to talk about?"

"I need better coping mechanisms," she told him. "Back in the day, it was drugs. Then, it was dick. Now, I'm just sort of flailing around with no distractions and it's like," She grimaced. "Not awesome."

"Well, there are several healthy ways to deal with stress. Meditation, exercise, healthy eating..."

"That all sounds really terrible."

He arched an eyebrow. "All right, in that case, what you need to do is get to the root of what's causing you to feel upset."

"Well, right now I'm freaking out because I had a big fight with my girlfriend. I've never been in a real relationship before. Intimacy issues, fear of abandonment, and a general lack of interest have made them seem like a giant pain in the ass. But, this girl's amazing and I think I fucked it up by lying to her and I'm afraid I won't be able to fix it."

"Was the lie to conceal infidelity?"

"No, I didn't tell her about someone stopping by her place one night. They were involved in something that I thought might be dangerous for her, so I sent them away. She found out, now she's mad."

He lowered his glasses and put his pen down. "That's it?"

"Yeah."

"You tried to protect her from a shady character and that upset her?"

Wyatt sat forward. "Did you just say 'shady'?"

Gabriel nodded.

The doctor placed his glasses and notebook on the table and leaned back in his seat. "Give it a few days. She'll get over it. If she doesn't, she's too immature for an adult relationship and you're better off without her."

Wyatt burst out laughing. "I am *loving* this new you."

She twirled her hair and crossed her legs. "Should I buy her something big, like a house or a car or something? Some kind of grand gesture to smooth it over?"

The doctor shook his head. "That's not necessary. What she probably needs is a sincere apology. Money doesn't solve every problem and you can't just buy people."

She cocked her head, glancing at the money on the table.

He cleared his throat. "Touche."

Chapter 12

Eight-year-old Wendy let out a blood-curdling scream as her parents were gunned down in front of her, the man with the rifle having smashed through the front door like a SWAT team member on crystal meth. Her mother was dead before she hit the floor and her father writhed in a pool of blood on the cream-colored carpet.

"Why?" he gurgled as the gunman stood over him.

He sneered, his thick mustache glistening in the bright sunlight that poured in through the hole where the door used to be. "Thou shalt not suffer a witch to live."

"I'm not a witch," he defended. "My powers were stripped when I was a baby."

"Not you." He altered his gaze to the girl who now hyperventilated in the corner.

"No!" her father begged. "She's just a little girl!"

He raised the rifle, pointing it at the girl. "Witches are never children. They're born evil. If you could go back and kill Stalin in his crib, wouldn't you?"

"Wendy, run!"

The man turned his gun back on her father and shot him between the eyes. Wendy screamed again, buckets of tears falling from her sorrowful eyes. The shooter pointed his weapon at her again but before he could pull the trigger, Wendy shouted, "Calidi!" The metal of the weapon instantly burned hot, searing the skin of his hand. He dropped the gun, crying out in pain. She took a few quick breaths and reminded herself, "I'm a witch. I'm a witch. I can do *anything. I'm a witch.*"

"I'm gonna kill you, you little bitch!"

She wiped away her tears and pointed to the man's left eye. "Dissilio!" It burst in his head, exploding like an over-filled water balloon. He howled, his charred hand flying up to cover the mess dribbling from his eye socket. While he was distracted, she made a break for it, speeding by him and out the door.

She raced through the field across the street and into the woods. She kept running to the other side of the forest to her grandmother's cottage, her tears again streaming down her now flushed cheeks.

"What's happened?" the old woman fretted, meeting Wendy on the front porch and cupping her small face in her wrinkled hands.

"The man," she panted. "Had a gun. He broke in. He killed them!" She began to sob, throwing her arms around her grandmother's waist.

She caught a breath in her throat. "My Daniel?"

"He said we're evil. Are we bad, Grandma?"

"No, sweetheart," the woman told her, brushing her own tears from her eyes and patting her on the back. "Just different. Some men fear what they can't control and that fear drives them to villainy." She knelt down to look her in the eyes. "You're a good girl, Wendy. But, no matter what you do or where you go, there will always be men who want to extinguish your power and witches that want to take it for themselves. You'll have to be guarded and careful, always. Promise me."

She gulped back a sob and nodded. "I promise, Grandma. What do I do now? I'm all alone."

She took her in her arms and squeezed her tight. "You're not alone. I'll always be with you, my sweet girl. I'll always be right here."

Shots rang out, dozens of bullets crashing through every window of the cabin as the witches inside shrieked, some ducking for cover while others perished instantly from bullets to the head or heart. The barrage continued as four men armed to the teeth busted through the door, their assault weapons smoking as they sprayed the women with round after round. When the screaming stopped, their leader held a fist in the air, signaling the others to hold their fire. He ran his fingers over his graying mustache before adjusting his eyepatch and taking stock of the carnage. He could make out eleven bodies strewn across the floor, the sight delighting him, but leaving him yet unsatisfied.

"We're missing one," he barked. "Fan out. Bitch has got to be here somewhere."

The men tore through the cabin, tossing furniture around as they stepped over the corpses of the fallen witches.

"You hear that?" one of the men asked. The group went quiet as they listened.

They heard what sounded like whispering, the same three words repeated over and over. "Caedis haec homines."

"Where's it coming from?" he asked.

"Stay frosty, boys," the leader said, raising his rifle. They looked everywhere, but couldn't find the source of the chanting. It got louder, echoing through the room as if it was being piped through a speaker system. The one-eyed man held his breath as he listened, cocking his head, a vicious smirk crossing his lips. He hoisted his gun straight up, squeezing the trigger, a single bullet releasing from the chamber. Above them, the woman yelped, blood dripping from her stomach wound onto the leader's shoulder. The men took aim, but the older man again made a fist. The witch had pinned herself to the ceiling using a flight spell, but as she bled out, she grew too weak to maintain it. She fell, landing with a thud on the floor in front of them. The leader laughed, holding his rifle in one hand and dragging the witch by her hair with the other. He threw her up against the wall in a sitting position, her skin already having lost most of its color. He knew he only had a couple of minutes to get the information from her before she was dead, so he wasted no time in questioning her. "Hey," he shouted, smacking her across the face to perk her up. "Dyer bitch. Don't conk out on me, yet. What's going on in your community of vipers, hmm?"

"What?" she breathed, barely able to keep her eyes open.

"Must be something big. Word has it the Gowdies left their compound and headed to New York. Now, why would they do something like that? I've had eyes on them for years and they never leave their little corner of the world, so what's so important that the entire coven would up and take a trip like that?"

"Caedis haec homines." Her head slumped as she began to fade.

"Oh, no you don't." He smacked her again, holding her head up, his fist gripping her hair. "What are they after? What's got you bitches all in a tizzy?"

"Wendy," she laughed.

"What? Did you say, 'Wendy'?"

"The Tituban." Blood slipped from her lips as her eyes rolled back. "She's the last. She contains all of her ancestors' power." She flashed a blood-stained smile as she coughed. "You may kill me, but you are all dead. She will discover what you've done and she will make you suffer. She'll skin you alive and hang you by your--"

"Wendy? Why does that name sound familiar?" He scratched underneath his eyepatch and laughed as the memory surfaced. "The kid?! Oh, I'm looking forward to this."

"Caedis haec homines."

"Are you doing a spell?" he cackled. "Yeah, those don't affect us anymore. A couple years back, we paid one of your kind to ward us from magic...right before we slit her throat."

Her eyes widened as they glossed over, a final, gurgling breath escaping her lips as her body went limp.

"Well done, boys," he said, standing upright and patting one of his men on the shoulder. "This coven is officially destroyed."

The men cheered, shooting their guns in the air and giving each other high-fives.

"No time to celebrate," the one-eyed man told them, heading for the door. "We've got a witch to hunt."

Chapter 13

Hartley leaned back, closing her eyes as she breathed in the salty ocean air, grateful for the shade the boardwalk above provided from the late-day sun. She sat comfortably on the blanket, digging her toes in the cool sand as she reflected on the events of the day. In the last twelve hours, she'd gone from vampire to human, single to having a live-in boyfriend, and from hating her mother to feeling sorry for and disturbed by her. "What a day."

"Fries for the lady," Oliver said, joining her on the blanket and opening a take-out container. She took one, dipping it in cheese sauce and taking a bite.

"Holy shit."

"Aren't they great? I've discovered any food tastes delicious if it's been deep-fried and covered in cheese." He took one as well, looking out onto the waves.

"Can I ask you something?"

"Anything, darling."

"Did your parents know you were...you know..."

"What? Pan?"

She nodded, taking another bite.

"I think they suspected."

"You never told them?"

"They never asked."

She raised an eyebrow.

He turned to face her. "I never told them because it seemed like they would have rather not known. Talking about things like sexuality just wasn't done then."

"Oh."

"What's the matter? Is someone giving you shit? Just give me a name."

She shook her head. "I went to visit my mom today."

He looked surprised. "You did? She's still alive?"

"Not for long from the looks of her. I don't know, I just..."

He held her hand. "What?"

"My parents did everything they could think of to change me. They made me feel worthless and ugly and...unloved. They hurt me. I don't know if I can forgive her."

He kissed her hand and held it to his chest. "Maybe you don't have to. Maybe it's not about her."

"What do you mean?"

"I mean, it's been decades since you've seen her, right?"

She nodded.

"And, if you never saw her again, how would that affect you, really?"

She shrugged.

"So, maybe forgiving what she did isn't necessary. Maybe all you need is closure."

"How do I get that?"

"Beats me," he said taking another fry and popping it in his mouth. He chewed and swallowed before speaking again. "But, whatever it is you need to do, you do it. No second-guessing, no stifling yourself for somebody else's comfort. You do whatever it takes to bring yourself peace because no matter what some old woman or anyone else might think of you, you deserve to be happy exactly the way you are."

She looked at him fondly as he kissed her hand again. "You know what?"

"What?"

"You might be the best decision I've made in years. Well, second best."

"All I felt was a huge spike in Julia's power," Poe said, crunching leaves under her biker boots as they trekked through the dense woods.

"I felt it, too, but that wasn't just Julia's magic getting stronger," Wendy told her. "There was something dark attached to it. Something old. If I'm right, we are in a pig farm's amount of shit." They came to the clearing, the faint smell of sulfur still lingering in the air.

"What the hell happened?" Poe asked, seeing the uprooted tree stump surrounded by centuries of silt and sandy loam.

Wendy furrowed her brow as she spotted the brass figure in a pile of leaves, split apart, a crack running through its center from the top down. All seven chambers had been unlocked. "Mother--"

"What is that thing?"

"Grace never told you the Moloch story?" She knelt down to gather up the candles and the rest of Tituba's belongings.

"No."

She stood and glanced around to make sure she hadn't left anything. "Back in the day, some girl summoned some kind of monster to get it to bring her dead relatives back to life. It demanded a human sacrifice, so the girl offered up Tituba's daughter. Tituba stopped her and trapped the monster in this idol. Some guy called it 'Moloch'."

"What guy?"

"I don't know. Tituba just referred to him as 'The Bringer of Light'." Her eyes widened and her mouth fell open. "You've got to be kidding me."

"Bringer of Light? Like--"

"Lucifer, yeah, probably. Oh, my God! I can't believe I never put that together before."

"What do we do now?" Poe asked. "The idol's broken. It's useless."

"It doesn't matter. That thing's been locked up so long, it can't function on its own. It needs a witch to act as a conduit. Without Julia's magic to cling to, it's nothing. All we have to do is take her power."

"Like with the Gowdies?"

"No, not bind it. Remove it completely. The stripping spell done on male witches when they're babies, *that's* what we need."

"We'd need her measure."

"I know." She began the long walk out of the woods, Poe following closely behind. "We'll need the coven."

Chapter 14

Allydia sat across from Phindi in the quiet 116th Street restaurant, watching her eat as she took a sip of Bissap. "How is your Fataya?"

"Fine," she mumbled. "How are your Nems?"

"Lovely. I had forgotten how much I used to love food. You know, for as long as I'd gone without it, I don't think it ever occurred to me to miss it."

She slammed her fist down on the table, startling the people at the next table. "This man, are you certain he is worth all of this? That he is worthy of you?"

She set her glass down and folded her hands. "I didn't do this only for him. I spent thousands of years trying to fix what was broken in me, creating a family to replace the one my father had taken. No matter how many of you I turned, there was always something missing."

She lowered her head. "We were not enough."

"No, because the thing that was missing was *me*. I had forgotten who I was. I lost myself somewhere between responsibility and repetition. I was *tired*, Phindi. But, to answer your question, yes, he is worth it. He is worth all the stars in heaven. More precious than any diamond. I would give my life to remain in his favor and I would burn this world to the ground to bring justice to anyone who might dare try to take him from me, do you understand?"

She nearly choked on her last bite of food as she nodded. "Yes, my Queen."

"Good." Her eyes softened. "I know it's hard, adjusting to this human life. I will help you in any way you need."

"What I *need* is purpose."

Allydia picked up her glass. "We will think of something."

"So, since Allydia's human now, are we just gonna forgive her for that whole locking-me-in-a-cage thing?"

Michelle asked, sitting next to Will on the couch in his father's apartment.

"That's entirely up to you," he told her. "I'll hate her if you want me to."

She sank back into the cushions and crossed her legs. "Your dad really loves her, doesn't he?"

"Yeah, I think he really does."

She sighed, resting her head on his shoulder as he put his arm around her. "I guess I can let it go, but only because I think I could take her now."

He laughed. "That's very big of you."

"I know, right? I'm a goddamn saint." She giggled, wrapping an arm around his waist. "Will,"

He kissed her head. "Hmm?"

"I miss her."

He rested his cheek on top of her head, knowing they were no longer talking about the ex-vampire queen. "Me, too."

"I was serious earlier. I want her back."

He rubbed her shoulder. "I know."

"She was so happy. Safe. She loves it there, I could tell." She brushed away a stray tear as Will held her close. "I can't just uproot her, it would break her heart. And Valerie and Malik seem like good parents, right? I mean, they have to be. She loves them. She's got drawings she's done of them all over her room. Her whole life has been with them. It's just not fair." She wiped away more tears as they came, her voice going up an octave as she spoke through the sobs. "She's growing up so fast. *So fast* and we're missing it. We should be with her. We should be..." She covered her mouth, her crying now out of control. He kissed her head again then pulled away, taking his phone from his back pocket and calling his aunt.

"Hello?" Valerie answered.

"Hey, Aunt Valerie, it's Will. I want to apologize. I think I may have insulted Malik earlier. I kind of implied he wasn't ambitious enough."

She laughed. "Yeah, he said something about you making a comment."

"Is he mad?"

"No, sweetie. He laughed it off, said you're too young to know what you're talking about."

"Oh," he said, blowing by the insult. "Well, good...I guess. Listen, I know you don't know me that well and I don't exactly have the best track record when it comes to being, you know, *sane*, but I was wondering if I could ask a favor."

"Boy, you're family. That's all I need to know about you. Besides, if sanity was a prerequisite for speaking, everyone in this family would have to cut their tongues out. What do you need?"

"It's big."

"That's all right."

"Really big."

"Boy, I love you, but my patience is wearing thin."

"I was wondering if it might be okay if me and Michelle," He looked at her as she sat forward, head tilted as she listened.

"If you and Michelle what?"

"If we moved in with you?"

Michelle gasped, covering her mouth with one hand and holding her stomach with the other.

"We just miss Sinclair already," he continued. "And, I don't mean we want to take over or anything. You and Malik are her parents, we just," He placed a hand on his girlfriend's knee. "We just want to be part of it."

"Daddy!" he could hear Sinclair squeal in the background. "Tell him yes, Mommy! Tell Daddy it's okay! Please?!"

Valerie laughed. "Well, I don't have a choice, now, do I?"

"Are you sure?" Will asked, not wanting to get his hopes up for nothing. "I know it's weird."

"Oh, sweetie, weird is so normal for this family, we should put it on a crest. Pack your stuff. I'll have a room ready for you."

"Thank you, Valerie. You have no idea how much this means to us."

"I'll see you soon."

"Yes, you will. Thank you. Bye." He hit 'end call' and put the phone on the coffee table. Michelle sat, jaw agape, eyes fixed on this man, this love of her life. She stared, eyes wide as he noticed her gawking. "Oh, God, did I overstep?" he wondered. "I did. I made a decision for both of us without asking you first. I'm sorry. Is that not what you wanted? I can call her back. I can--"

"Will," she breathed.

"What?"

"Will you marry me?"

"Yes."

"Really? You don't need a second to think about it?"

"Wait, do you mean tonight or ever? Yes to either."

She laughed. "How about this weekend?"

"Yes." He took her face in his hands and kissed her before resting his forehead on hers. "The answer will always be yes. Anything you want, for the rest of my life, you'll have it. I'm gonna give you everything."

Chapter 15

Hey, Gabriel thought to Lucifer. *You busy?*

He scanned the bar for potential playmates. The room was full of beautiful women, but two, in particular, caught his fancy. Both had long, dark hair, their full lips and easy smiles reminding him of Mariana. They sat huddled together in a booth, laughing over the rims of their martini glasses. *Yes.*

Will wants us at B's place. Says he has an announcement. Meet us there?

He smirked as he headed for the table. *Can't. I'm on the prowl.* "Hello, ladies. Mind if I join you?"

They giggled, the one on the left patting the seat next to her.

"Is he coming?" Wyatt asked as he opened the door to his apartment and waited for her to enter before going in himself.

"No," she grumbled. "Says he's busy."

"Doing what?"

"Ho-ing."

"Hey!" Will cheered, pouring them flutes of sparkling cider. "Where have you been? We're celebrating!"

They took the glasses, Gabriel laughing under her breath as she took a sip of the fizzy beverage. Michelle rushed over, Will wrapping his arm around her as she stood next to him.

"Celebrating what?" Wyatt asked.

Michelle beamed, holding up her left hand, showing off the two-carat, white gold halo engagement ring. "We're getting married!"

"Sunday," Will chimed.

"And, we're moving in with Valerie to be close to Sinclair."

"Come eat! I made a ton of food." The couple scampered to the kitchen, Wyatt remaining motionless in the entry.

"You're freaking out," Gabriel said.

"Little bit."

She laughed. "They'll be fine. I can't see in *his* head, but she's all about him. Honestly, who are we to judge? It's a healthier relationship than either of ours."

"You got me there." They clinked glasses. "Where'd he get the money for that ring?"

"I gave him a credit card."

"Of course you did."

"What?"

He shook his head.

"Don't give me shit. I've had a very hard day."

He laughed. "All right. So, you gonna apologize to Wendy?"

"Probably. I should give her a little space first, though, right? She was pretty pissed."

"Yeah, let her cool off a little."

"Yeah."

"Guys!" Will called. "Get in here! I made steak and lava cake."

"He said lava cake," Gabriel bubbled, rushing toward the kitchen.

Wyatt laughed as he followed, taking another sip of cider and joining the others around the island.

Gabriel raised her glass. "To Will and Michelle." They all clinked glasses and began to eat. "So, how offended will you be if I don't eat the asparagus? Like, you'll still give me the cake, right?"

Will chuckled. "Yeah, Aunt Gabriel. You can still have cake. And, I made you two."

She pinched his cheek. "That's why I love you, kid."

Lucifer gazed out the hotel room window, the newly-darkened sky reflecting his feelings of emptiness as he succumbed to his melancholy. Even with two women on top of him, one gyrating on his genitals, the other behind her, kissing her neck and fondling her breasts, he couldn't help but feel bored. Perhaps he'd cared more for Mariana than he'd let himself admit. He let out a mournful sigh and put his hands behind his head. "It's not the same."

Allydia and Phindi stood outside of the four-story building on Wooster and Broome, its black steps leading to the glass storefront glistening under the light of the pale moon.

"What do you think?" the former queen asked. "Gym on the first floor, offices on the third. You could live on the fourth and teach self-defense on the second."

"I don't know," Phindi said, hugging her arms against the cool evening breeze. "Running a business? I wouldn't know where to begin."

"Then you'll hire a manager, someone with experience to run day-to-day operations while you focus on instructing."

"And, you are sure there is a need?"

"I am. Hartley reminded me today of the brutality of men. As long as humanity persists, there will be a need for those who are seen as weak to learn to protect themselves from the strong. You've been my fiercest warrior, but now, the fighting is done. Put your skills to a worthy purpose. You protected my kingdom. Now, teach others to protect themselves."

Phindi looked up to the fourth-floor windows and back down to the storefront, a single potted plant sitting outside of its black-trimmed windows; life against the brick and mortar. She dipped her head then turned to face her former queen. "Then, I accept this challenge. I will make you proud."

"I know that, Phindi. You always do."

Chapter 16

Emergency. Meet at the covenstead NOW.

Donna read the group text from Poe and put her phone in her back pocket before walking down the steps to her basement. The open, mostly empty room had served as the coven's meeting place since Grace's death and while it was conveniently located in her own house, it also meant that she was now in possession of and responsible for all of the coven's most sacred belongings. It was an honor but a burden, knowing that if anything should happen to her home, whether it be fire or flood, the coven's most important items would also be lost. Still, she'd been humbled by her sisters' confidence in her and did her best to ensure the safety of their grimoires, potions, and measures, the last being arguably the most important things a coven retained. The knotted cords functioned as talismans for each witch in the coven, giving the group the ability to control or even kill its members. They were symbols of loyalty, binding each witch to the rest in perfect love and perfect trust. She kept them in a fireproof safe built into the wall opposite the door along with the other sacred objects just as her fallen Priestess had when they resided in *her* home.

"Donna,"

She jumped, startled as she turned to see Julia standing in the corner. "You aren't welcome here anymore."

"I'm giving you a chance to reconsider."

"Reconsider what? Shunning you? I won't." She studied her as she became aware of her increase in power. It was significant and something about it was off. It felt malevolent and as she stepped closer, the odd scent of sulfur filled her nose, making her queasy. "What did you do?"

A sly grin crept across her face. "What I had to." She closed the space between them and as she drew closer, Donna became lightheaded, needing to steady herself against the wall. "You feel it, don't you?" Julia gleaned. "The power?"

She went ghost white, sweat forming on her temples. "What have you done?" She swallowed the bile coming up in her throat and she fought to regulate her breathing. "What I feel coming from you isn't human. What have you attached yourself to?"

"It doesn't matter. I can take it back for us. I have everything we need to take Grace's magic by force. Make me Priestess. I'll lead this coven in a new, glorious age. We'll put the Dyers to shame. The Gowdies will be *nothing* compared to us. Give me control and there will be nothing we can't do."

"I don't know what dark entity you've gotten mixed up with, but even with its help, you are no match for a Tituban witch. It's time for you to go." She opened her mouth wide, releasing a low vibration that pulsed through the room.

Julia squeezed her eyes shut as the wave went through her, causing her diaphragm to seize and her lungs to empty themselves of air with no way of taking in more. A gust of wind began to push Julia backward, her heels dragging across the wooden planks as she fought to hold her ground. After a few seconds of getting her bearings, she planted her feet, cracking her neck and opening her eyes to reveal the now glistening obsidian spheres, like black lacquer pools where her eyes used to be. She flittered her fingers toward the ground as she grinned, conjuring up dozens of snakes. They slithered their way to Donna, wrapping themselves around her ankles and up her legs.

"Evanescet," Donna commanded, but the snakes remained.

"You're the most powerful in our circle and your magic is useless against me." Julia stepped toward her. "You should have accepted me."

The older witch clenched her jaw and turned, stumbling toward the safe.

"What are you gonna do?" Julia scoffed. "Hit me with a lust potion?" But, as she opened the safe, a knot of dread formed in her stomach. As Donna reached inside, Julia whispered, "My measure." She screamed, lifting off her feet and flying toward her. She knocked her to the ground, climbing on top of her and wrestling the cord away. She pinned her down while serpents of varying species slid over her body. Donna's blood pressure dropped and her heart-rate sped out of control as the stench of sulfur overwhelmed her. Julia licked her lips, seeming to get a twisted pleasure from her former sister's panic as an eight-foot black Mussurana glided up Donna's body to her throat, wrapping itself around her neck and beginning the constriction. Her face went blue and her eyes bulged as the blood vessels in the sclera burst, turning red what was once white. Julia exhaled, getting to her feet as the snakes disappeared underneath the floorboards, their job done. Donna was dead, leaving the coven even weaker than before.

Julia threaded her measure through her fingers as she hovered over the fresh corpse, her eyes returning to their original shade. The coven would never accept her now. That was fine. She didn't need them. She'd take Grace's power for herself and if anyone got in her way, they'd just have to die, too.

Wendy and Poe found the coven waiting for them in Donna's basement. They sat in a crescent, Donna's body under a sheet on the floor in front of them. Most were still in tears, but Nicole was stone-faced and ready for revenge. She got up to meet them, putting herself between them and the body.

Poe gasped. "Donna?"

Nicole nodded. "Linda did some candle scrying. Julia took her measure and killed her. It was Julia but also something...*else*. You can still feel it. It's dark."

"I know what it is," Wendy told her. "I know it feels like it's super powerful, but it's been locked up for centuries. It's barely functioning. It needs a witch to latch onto or else it's basically just a creepy shadow."

"Julia wants Grace's magic," Linda said from her seat, her hands trembling. "I saw her intentions in the flame. She wants to take us over," She looked Wendy in the eyes. "And kill you."

She smacked her lips. "Things have been trying to kill me my whole life, but your girl's still here. I'm sorry about your friend." She returned her gaze to Nicole. "No one else is dying today."

"You didn't see what I saw," Linda choked, sniffing and wiping her cheek with the back of her sleeve.

Wendy's expression turned hard. "Get in a circle." She knelt down and opened her bag, taking out Tituba's white candles. The women looked at each other and shrugged before standing and forming a circle. She placed the candles around them and began lighting them.

Poe knelt next to her. "What are you doing?"

"Get in the circle, Poe," she ordered.

Her tone made the girl's heart jump. She got up, standing with her sisters as they watched. The women grew nervous as Wendy stepped over Donna's body to pick up a chair and move it to the center of the circle. She stood on it and took a deep breath. They looked up at her, joining hands and exchanging worried glances.

"What's the plan?" Poe asked.

Wendy rolled her neck then cracked her knuckles. "Bait and fucking switch."

Chapter 17

Lucifer downed his third beer of the hour and tapped his napkin signaling for more. The bartender reluctantly poured him another. "Last one, man."

Lucifer took a sip and put the glass down. "I assure you, I can handle it."

"If you say so. You wanna talk about it?"

"About what?"

"Whatever's got you drinkin'?"

He put his elbows on the bar and thought for a moment. "I think I've been here too long."

"Aight. Let me call you a cab."

"Not here at the bar. On Earth. I've allowed myself attachments. I've acquired disappointment. What's worse is that I find myself without purpose. No enemy to battle. No demon to put back in his place. No evil to vanquish. No part to play in a Divine plan. I'm simply *here*. How do you people do it?"

He cocked his head and raised an eyebrow. "Us people?"

"Yes, humans. You go bumbling through life with no direction, no instruction, aside from the educations provided to you by other humans which is mediocre at best and offensive in its ignorance. And, when you do manage to formulate a plan, more often than not it gets torn to shreds by forces out of your control. How do you go on every day as if it's all fine?" He took another drink. "I'm beginning to have a new appreciation for my brother's repeated attempts at ending his misery once and for all." He took another swig as the bartender sighed.

"I did not need this today," he muttered to himself. "Listen, man, I don't know what you're going through, but taking yourself out isn't a thing to do. If you can't give a shit about yourself, think about the people you'd be leaving behind."

He fiddled with his glass, watching the amber fluid as it swirled. "My sister *would* be quite upset with me. Well, one of them. The other would be indifferent, I imagine. You know, I have no idea how my brother would react. For all the times he's tried to murder me, I think he's starting to come around." He looked up at him. "Honestly, how do you live these lives of constant failures, mistakes, and tragedies?"

"Listen, man, life can fuck you over. A lot. No doubt. But, you keep pushin', keep chippin' away at whatever that goal is. What choice you got? Lay down and die? I don't know about you, but my momma didn't raise a little bitch. So, I'm gonna get my ass up every mornin' and get to work, and if I never get what I want outta life, at least when I get to the pearly gates I can say I gave it everything I had. I kept my nose clean, I treated people decent, and I did everything I could. At the end of the day, it don't matter how many times you get knocked down. What matters is how many times you get back up."

Lucifer tapped his fingers to his lips. "That's very wise." He stood and shook the man's hand. He was preparing to go when a patron shuffled up behind him, blocking his path.

"Hey, boy," the man gruffed. "Get me another whiskey."

Lucifer turned his head to see the drunk, then looked back at the bartender whose jaw had become tight. He leaned in, speaking as quietly as could be heard in the noisy bar. "'Boy' is still a slur, is it not? I've heard my sister call my nephew that, but he's as white as they come. It's a bit confusing. You look perturbed, so I'm assuming it's still offensive, yes?"

The bartender nodded as he wrung his hands, his whole body visibly tense.

"Well, then," Lucifer shot back his elbow, slamming it into the racist's face, shattering his nose and knocking him out cold. He finished his beer and set the glass down, grinning as the bartender lifted his eyes and put his fist to his mouth. Lucifer paid his tab and leaned on the bar. "Would you like me to kill him for you?"

Allydia got back to Wyatt's as Will and Michelle sat down to watch the eleven o'clock news. "Children," she greeted.

"Hey," Will said. "I saved you a plate. It's in the oven. You might want to start with the cake, though. Gabriel's on a sugar bender."

"Isn't she always? Thank you, Will. And, thank you for your assistance with Phindi earlier."

"Everything okay there?"

"Yes, fine. She was just feeling a little lost, needed some direction."

"Hey," Wyatt said as he came into the room, giving Allydia a quick kiss. "Did they tell you?"

"Tell me what?"

Michelle sat forward and held out her hand to show her the engagement ring.

Allydia looked to Wyatt to gauge his reaction before making a judgement. He shoved his hands in his pockets and lifted his eyebrows as he simpered. She shifted her gaze back to the couple and smiled. "Well, congratulations."

"Thank you," Michelle beamed, patting Will on the knee to get his attention. "Let's go shopping for Sinclair's flower girl dress tomorrow. I don't want to put it off to the last minute."

"Who's Sinclair?" The room went quiet, all three of them looking bug-eyed at her, Michelle covering her mouth in regret at what she'd let slip.

"It's fine," Gabriel called from the island as she finished her second piece of cake. "B, maybe take her in the other room to tell her, though. She might react badly. But, I mean, she's human now. What's she gonna do, complain?"

"Come on," Wyatt said, taking her hand and leading her into his bedroom. He closed the door and stood in front of it as she cleared her throat.

"Wyatt," she hesitated, folding her arms and doing her best to keep from looking agitated.

"It's all right."

"It doesn't feel all right."

"I'm sorry," he told her. "I couldn't tell you. Gabriel said you would have killed her."

"Did you…" She dug her nails into her arms as she tried to hold it together. "When Will was a child and we were apart…"

"Oh, no! No, I didn't…she's not *mine*."

She let out a sigh of relief and relaxed her shoulders.

"She's Will's."

She stared at him blankly. "What?"

"His and Michelle's. Michelle was a vampire when she had her, so Gabriel thought you'd--"

"Get out of my way."

"Calm down."

"How old is she, in appearance?"

"About seven. Why?"

"She hasn't come into her full power, yet. There's still time."

"We're not *killing her*, Allydia."

"You've never dealt with something like this," she warned. "Human/vampire hybrids aren't like other vampires. Vampires kill for food or in passion. Their emotions were nearly impossible to keep in check. Hybrids are calculating, premeditated."

"Sounds like someone else I know."

She bit her lip. "I did what I had to to keep my people in line. These things--"

"She's not a *thing*. She's my granddaughter. She's a sweet little girl that likes to draw and go to the park. She's a kid."

"So was Hitler, once. Had I known what he'd become when I met him, I would have killed him, too."

He did a double-take. "You met Hitler?"

"Briefly. He was in a waiting room at a hospital in Linz when I was there for...dinner. He was a teenager, I think. I didn't pay much attention. He was no one at the time. Listen to me, Wyatt. Hybrids are the most powerful creatures on Earth. They can survive almost anything once they mature. If we wait too long, there will be nothing we can do."

"Allydia,"

"They get hyper-focused. Fixated. They set a goal and nothing will keep them from achieving it."

"You sure we're not talking about you?"

She cast him a condescending glare. "Hybrids alone are methodical and cunning serial killers with no capacity for remorse or empathy. Pair that with what you know a Nephilim to be and tell me you're not at all concerned."

He sighed and crossed his arms. "Gabriel says she's okay."

"Well, you'll have to excuse my unwillingness to put too much faith in your sister's judgement after she let your son live."

He stared daggers at her.

"I'm sorry. I'm happy that it all worked out. I am. I've come to appreciate Will and he obviously loves you very much, but you know what he was. Imagine that at ten times the power and with foresight." Hot tears formed in the corners of her eyes as she stepped closer. "When she gets to full power, I will be useless in a fight. I'm human. I won't be able to protect you."

His eyes softened and he cupped her face in his hands. "I don't need you to protect me. I've got a family of archangels for that."

She laughed, wiping a tear from her cheek.

He smiled. "Nothing's gonna happen to me, okay? Sinclair's not dangerous. If she was, Gabriel probably would have killed her without ever telling me she existed, right?"

"Maybe."

He kissed her. "Everything will be fine, I promise."

She nodded, unconvinced.

From the kitchen, Gabriel side-eyed the bedroom door as she took a sip of soda.

"Everything okay?" Will asked from the couch.

She snapped to attention. "Yeah. Everything's fine." She peered at the door again, taking another long sip and placing the can back on the counter. "Everything's gonna be just fine."

Chapter 18

Wendy trekked through the dense foliage of the forest floor, the cool night air still like an undisturbed lake. Poe had described a small clearing at the center of the woods behind Grace's house where her great-aunt had performed her sacred rituals and most difficult spells. Wendy headed to the spot, hoping to tap into any residual energy that might have been left there.

The pale light of the quarter moon was barely visible through the just-turning leaves of the towering oak trees. In the distance, she could hear the caw of a crow as the branches above her began to tremor. She stopped, peering up into the darkness. After a few seconds, the figure of a woman crouching in the tree became clear and from above her Wendy could hear the quiet command. "Transuerso."

She giggled. "Hey, you *are* strong. That almost tickled."

Julia hopped to a lower branch, her face now visible. "Tranuerso!"

"Won't work," Wendy told her. "You wanna come down here? I'm starting to get a crick in my neck."

"TRANSUERSO!"

She sighed. "What's it gonna be? Big fight or save us some time and just toss me the measure now?"

Incensed, Julia leaped from the tree, flinging herself onto Wendy and knocking her to the ground. She smacked her, first with her right hand, then her left.

"Subsisto!"

Julia's hands became immobile at Wendy's command. "I will have your power," she seethed as the forest floor began to move, every inch as far as her eyes could see now lousy with snakes.

Wendy shuddered at the sight of them. "Well, that's not what you want. Sursum." She rose up, sending Julia staggering backward.

"Da mihi!" Julia demanded.

"You know what? I don't think I will."

Her eyes shined black, reflecting the moonlight like onyx glass. She lifted off the ground, hovering above her as she spread her arms open wide. Thunder clapped as thirty-mile-an-hour winds pelted the landscape with hail. "Deditionem tuus potentia!"

"Nope."

Her face twisted in rage, her chest heaving. "Morietur!"

"*Die*? Really? That's rude." Wendy unfurled the measure she'd swiped from Julia's pocket.

"How did you get that?!"

"Nicked it when you were taking your frustrations out on my face. Did you really think I'd let you hit me for no reason? You girls ready?"

"Ready." Poe emerged from the trees, taking the cord and rushing it back to Nicole's awaiting hands just a few feet away in Grace's clearing. Linda lit the candles as Nicole began fraying the edges of the measure.

Julia gasped. "Where did they come from? Why couldn't I feel their magic?"

"I worked one of Tituba's spells. My grandma used it on me when I was a kid to protect me from, well, people like you. From now on, no one outside of the coven will recognize them as witches."

Linda lit the last candle and began to chant, "Praesidio in loco isto."

"No!" Julia flew toward them but was repelled by an invisible wall. She watched in horror as Nicole pulled a single strand from the cord and drop it into the silver ritual bowl. She turned back to Wendy, jaw clenched, and face flushed. "You'll pay."

Wendy scrunched her nose. "Will I, though?"

"MORIETUR!"

"Have you still not figured this out? I'm warded. I can't be spelled."

A sinister smirk appeared on her lips as she pulled the Catseye from her pocket.

"What is that?" Wendy asked, squinting to see.

"You should have checked both pockets."

She stepped closer, still unable to make out the small object in the dark.

"You can't ward yourself from your own blood. Coquito."

Wendy felt a rush of heat flow through her, starting at her heart and making its way through her entire circulatory system. She fell to her knees as Julia cackled. "Cook," she choked, her hand resting on her chest as she began to panic, the realization of what was happening causing her mind to race. She was dying and there was nothing she could do to stop it. Her blood was boiling in her veins.

She dropped onto her back, snakes slithering up her legs and over her abdomen. Her skin turned beet-red as she began to sweat. *I should have forgiven Gabriel*, she thought. *I shouldn't have pushed her away.*

"AUFERETUR!" Poe yelled, running between the women, her eyes sparkling like emeralds. Julia was thrown into the trees, Poe rocketing up to meet her. The two clashed, clawing at each other like jackals as they slammed into branches, careening through the air like out-of-control space junk. They plummeted to the ground like meteors, cratering the forest floor, spewing dirt and snake pieces in all directions.

Julia got the upper hand, pinning the sixteen-year-old in the depression with her mind as she herself floated out, a satisfied sneer on her pale lips. "Your power may be increased, but you are *nothing* compared to me. You're a child out of her depth. You should have stayed in hiding. Operculum!"

The ground beneath her began to rumble as she struggled to break free of Julia's spell. The walls of soil around her crumbled, filling the pit, and entombing the young witch.

Julia laughed, turning her attention back to the coven as she stepped over Wendy lying screaming in agony on the grass. She held her hands out, using everything she had to penetrate the protection spell. Just as she was beginning to make progress, the sound of an explosion rang out from behind. She spun around and was confronted by a dirt-covered Poe, her eyes shining even more brightly than before.

"I may be a kid, but I can still whoop your ass." The girl waved a hand in her enemy's direction and bellowed, "Quercus!" Julia was hurled into a massive oak, her head bloodied on the bark as she collapsed unconscious to the forest floor.

Poe hurried to kneel next to Wendy who lay barely alive, wheezing and crying blood tears. "Amoveatur," she ordered, her eyes returning to normal.

Wendy coughed, gulping in air as the redness in her skin disappeared. She sat up, still too lightheaded to stand as her temperature went down. She patted her friend's arm and steadied her breathing. "Thanks, Poe."

Julia stood, her face twisted in rage as she touched the back of her head and looked at the blood on her hand when she pulled it away.

Wendy tried to stand, but her legs were like jelly. "I'm not really up to snuff. You got this?"

Poe hopped up and stretched her arms over her chest. "Yeah, I'm good."

Wendy crawled to join the others in the circle as Julia bounded forward.

"Adflicto!" Poe shouted, causing her adversary's spine to snap.

She fell but soon recovered, the monster inside her healing the break almost immediately. "Sursus deorsum!"

Poe was flung upside down in the air, hovering as if she were being held by her ankles.

"We have to hurry," Wendy asserted. Nicole dropped a match in the bowl, sending a green flame to jump then dissipate. She looked at the group, each one nodding to convey their readiness. In unison, the witches spoke the sacred words, "Nunc marcus finis eius magicae."

"NO!" Julia cried as her eyes lost their sheen. Tears poured down her cheeks as the air stilled, the clouds moved out, and the snakes slithered back to where they'd come from.

Poe crashed to the ground, released from the former witch's spell. Julia fell to her knees, powerless and devastated. She sobbed, covering her face with shaky hands as Nicole approached, her face like stone.

She looked down at her, hands clenched behind her back. "We banish you, Julia of the Kyteler line. You will leave the State of New York, never to return for any reason. And, let me make this crystal clear for you. If I ever see you again, I will kill you." She went back to her sisters, leaving Julia to cry alone. There was no coming back from this, no revenge to be had. She was nothing.

Chapter 19

Hartley listened to the waves crashing outside the Atlantic City apartment. She lay in bed, unnerved by how tired she already was as Oliver slept quietly next to her. Up until now, midnight had been her noon, her "day" barely started. Now, she could hardly keep her eyes open as the cool ocean breeze coming in through the open window filled the air with a clean saltiness, lulling her to sleep. These new hours would take some getting used to.

As she drifted off, her phone rang. She answered it quickly as not to disturb her new-ish boyfriend. "Yes?"

"Is this Hartley?" the woman on the other end asked.

"It is."

"Hello, doll. This is Wanda, your grandmother's nurse. I just wanted to let you know that Gloria passed peacefully in her sleep about an hour ago."

She sat up, her heart leaping to her throat.

"She was very happy to see you and your father today. I've never seen her smile that much."

"My father?"

"Yes. She said seeing her son again was the best gift she could've asked for. I must have missed him. Can you give him the news? I don't have a number for him. Thank God you left yours. Nothing's more tragic than learning about the death of a loved one in the obituaries."

"Um, of course. Yes, I'll tell him."

"Thank you, dear. Now, Father Daniel has been by to perform the last rites and has scheduled her service for three this Saturday at St. Anthony's. Will I see you there?"

"Um,"

A dog barked in the background. "Oh, shoot. Forgot to let the dog out. I have to go. I'm so sorry for your loss."

"Thank you." She ended the call and set the phone on the nightstand, lying back and pulling the sheets up to her chin. She stared up at the ceiling, unsure of how to feel. Her mind was swirling with the revelations of the day, her eyelids heavy. In his sleep, Oliver rolled over and threw an arm over her waist. She hugged it, grateful to have someone there with her. She fell asleep, unaware of the single tear that slid down her cheek.

The coven gathered in Grace's living room to discuss what to do now that Donna was gone. Wendy sat at the kitchen table, cuddling Raven as Poe made tea for the group. As she waited for the kettle, Poe took a seat next to her friend and folded her hands, pleading with her eyes.

"What?" Wendy asked, already knowing the answer.

"Well? Are you gonna join us, or what?"

"Or what."

She stuck out her lip.

"Don't give me that face," she giggled.

"We need you."

"You don't."

"Wendy,"

"Look, Poe, I understand how important covens can be. Aside from the occasional need for the power of multiple witches, the sisterhood, the bonds that you all have...it's awesome. I had that with my grandma back in the day. But, the coven is just...not where I belong."

She put her elbow on the table. "Where is, then? The city?"

"Probably."

"With Gabriel?"

She sighed and put the bunny on the table, petting its ears. "Feels that way."

"Well, you know we're always around if you need us."

"Same."

"Thank you, Wendy," Nicole said, entering the room and sitting across the table. "We appreciate everything you did for us today. If there's anything we can do to repay you in the future, don't hesitate to call."

She nodded.

"Poe, the girls have been talking. It may be unorthodox, but we would like *you* to be our new Priestess."

"What?" she coughed.

Wendy patted her back.

"Tonight, you proved yourself to be the most powerful among us. You showed bravery and compassion. And, Grace loved you like a daughter. It's only fitting that you should take her place."

She cleared her throat. "I don't know what to say."

"Say you'll do it," Wendy winked.

"I-I accept."

"Wonderful. I'll tell the others." She got up and went back to the living room as the kettle began to whistle. Wendy stood and poured the water into the teapot while Poe remained motionless, jaw agape.

Wendy sat back down, letting the tea steep. "You okay?"

"Not really."

She laughed. "You'll be fine. I have a feeling this is what Grace was grooming you for. I didn't know her, but if she was anything like her sister, she knew what she was doing."

"I'm only sixteen."

"All right, so, maybe that's not *ideal*." She laughed. "But, you have five sisters in there that love you and trust you. And, you have family in me."

"I do?"

She smacked her lips. "Girl, we're practically cousins."

She smiled and hugged her. "Thanks, Wendy."

"No problem. Hey, I think your rabbit's jealous."

They looked at the bunny now up on its hind legs, its front paws covering its face. They laughed as Poe picked it up, snuggling it under her chin. "You think you'll ever get a familiar?"

She considered it, conceding that Raven was super cute. "Maybe. One day."

Wendy knocked on Gabriel's door, but there was no answer. She tried opening it, but it was locked. She glanced around the hall. It was empty. "Recludo." The bolt unlocked and she let herself in. She went to the bedroom where she expected Gabriel to be sleeping, but it was empty. No one was home. She sat on the ottoman, tapping her fingers on the soft fabric, and waited.

Chapter 20

Will and Michelle lay unconscious in front of the TV, having fallen asleep during the monologue of a late-night talk show. Allydia, too, had gone to bed while Wyatt and Gabriel stayed up talking.

"You're not tired?" he asked.

"I am," she replied, spinning her empty soda can on the island.

"But, you don't want to go home."

"Not especially."

He sat next to her, arm on the counter as he faced her. "You're miserable. Maybe you should call her."

"It's not just that," she admitted. "It's all the things. God's work, secrets I have to keep. It's getting to be too much and I don't know how I'm gonna keep doing it."

"You'll do it, whatever it is because you have to. You always do. My friend Tim would say you have broad shoulders. Anything that gets put on them, you'll carry."

She looked away as she nodded in resentful agreement.

"But, it *is* okay to take a break once in a while."

She scoffed. "That hasn't been my experience."

He laughed. "All right, but you set yourself *on fire* today. You'd be dead if Lucifer hadn't saved you. Think about that sentence and tell me you don't need a break."

She laughed out loud. "Satan as a savior is pretty funny. Although, he *is* a good dude, just kind of fucked up."

"Yeah."

"He's growing on you."

He rolled his eyes.

"You care about him."

"Stop," he smirked.

She giggled. "He's your new best friend. You're gonna start having sleepovers and braiding each other's hair."

"Okay."

"It's nice. You *should* get along. He's a lot, but he loves you."

He looked amused. "He loves me?"

"Don't tell him I told you, but he's desperate for your approval. He sees you as a kind of moral authority. He respects you."

"Really?"

"He brought Will back because he couldn't stand to see you so upset. I know you remember how Barachiel feels about him."

He crossed his arms and sighed.

"You've been great friends basically since you were created. You just don't remember it."

"He's all right."

"Besties."

He shook his head.

"I'm gonna have necklaces made."

"Geez."

"No! Friendship bracelets."

"You need a nap."

Lucifer stumbled down the street, his buzz not quite inebriation. He took a swig from his nearly empty whiskey bottle, still in the bag it came in as not to alert police. He'd hoped to feel the effects of the alcohol more fully, but it would seem he hadn't had enough. He couldn't help but be disappointed in the bartender's refusal to take him up on his offer of bigot-homicide as he thought about the last time he'd taken his frustrations out on men who had offended a barkeep he'd come to admire. He finished the bottle and dropped it in a trashcan as he passed, wondering what kind of trouble he could get into before the night was through.

The streets were unusually quiet. Or was it just later than he thought? Only a few people walked by and street traffic moved freely, not a single traffic jam his entire walk. He took his phone from his pocket and checked the time. 2:07 AM. "Ah," he said to himself. He leaned against a lamppost and scrolled through his old messages, reading back conversations he'd had with Mariana that he hadn't been able to delete.

Ready for round two?
Of course!

Be there shortly.

Not the most romantic words ever written, but they plucked at his heartstrings all the same.

He replaced the phone and took in his surroundings. The lights, the vibrancy, the pollution. "I don't belong here." He shoved his hands in his pockets and began walking, aimless in the dark.

Chapter 21

The one-eyed man held a finger to his lips as he waved his men closer to the apartment door. "Remember, we're taking our time with this one. No shootin'. We're gonna do this old school."

The three men nodded, evil grins plastered on their faces as they rubbed their hands together in anticipation.

"Don't kill her, now. That's *my* right. Hurt her real bad, but *I* put the nail in the coffin."

Again, they nodded.

"Let's get to it, then." He kicked the door in, leaving a scuff mark where his boot hit.

Wendy shot up from her seat on the ottoman. Assuming they were burglars, she waved a hand at them. "Auferetur!" But, the men just laughed. "What the hell?"

"Wendy, right?" the leader asked, stepping forward.

"Foris!"

"That won't work on us. We took precautions."

"What do you want?"

He drew closer. "I know it's been some years, but, I was wondering, do you remember me?"

She studied the man's face as her heart pounded in her ears. She caught a breath in her throat as her bottom lip began to quiver.

"That's right."

"You killed my parents," she breathed.

"You took my eye. Some might call that square. I say, we have unfinished business."

Seeing that there was no way out, adrenaline coursing through her veins, she punched him in the mouth, causing drops of blood to spill from his lip to the floor.

He rubbed his face. "Oh, you're spunky, I'll give you that." He backhanded her, knocking her to the ground and kicking her in the abdomen. "Come on, boys. Time to teach this witch bitch a lesson."

They snickered and whooped as they bounded over, taking turns kicking her in the back and head. They pounded on her with their fists, one of them pinning her to the floor with his knee on her diaphragm. She couldn't breathe as blood poured from her mouth and broken nose. Her eyes swelled shut from repeated punches and her shattered ribs had punctured one of her lungs. She'd gone numb, probably from shock. She couldn't move, limp on the hardwood as the men continued their assault.

The one-eyed man shooed the others away as he straddled her waist and hit her again. "I'm gonna enjoy watching you die."

As he wrapped his thick fingers around her throat, she heard a familiar voice in the distance. "Well, well, well. I had planned on going straight to bed, but butchering a handful of intruders is probably just the thing I need to ensure a good night's rest."

"Mind your business, buddy," one of the men barked, pointing his rifle at him. Lucifer smirked and snatched it away, breaking it over his knee and discarding the pieces before headbutting the stunned witch hunter, rendering him unconscious.

"Who's next?"

The two foot-soldiers raised their weapons, spraying the room with bullets, Lucifer's body riddled with quick-healing wounds. He lunged at them, yanking the guns from their hands and tossing them to the ground. He picked one of the men up and threw him into a wall before smashing the other's head on the kitchen counter, crushing it like a rotted piece of fruit. The first man got to his feet and staggered toward him, Lucifer laughing at the determined look on his face.

He grabbed him by the collar and tossed him to the floor. "It was unwise of you to come to this place." He lifted his boot and slammed it down on the intruder's head, cracking his skull and killing him instantly. "And, then there's you." He stomped toward the man with the eyepatch, his cheeks crimson with rage at the sight of Wendy's condition.

"Who the hell are you?" the man shouted, standing up and pulling his pistol.

He rolled his head back. "So many titles. "Shining One. Light-Bearer. Watch-Keeper of the Damned. God's Strongest and, of course, Favorite of the Almighty."

His hand began to shake. "S-Sa--"

He gripped him by the throat with one hand while disarming him with the other. *"I am not Satan."*

The man grabbed his wrist, struggling to get free as he choked.

He pulled him close, teeth clenched as he spoke in a soft, deep tone. "My name is *Lucifer*." He spun him around and snapped his neck, dropping his body to the floor and brushing his hands together as he looked over the rest, making sure no man was left breathing. "I'd almost forgotten how much I enjoyed a good slaughter." His eyes fell to the broken witch. "Wendy," he whispered, falling to his knees next to her, holding her face in his hands as he inspected her head wounds. *Gabriel,*

Sup?

Wendy's hurt. Come home now. I fear she doesn't have much time.

Coming.

He tapped her cheek to try to coax her awake, but she was too far gone. He listened for a heartbeat. It was slow, her breathing rattled and shallow.

"Just sit tight," he pleaded. "Gabriel's on her way." But, there was no time. Her chest fell and didn't rise again. "Come on, love," He felt for a pulse but couldn't find one. "Must you be so impatient? I haven't healed anyone in sixty-five years and it never was my strong suit. Can you not hang on until Gabriel arrives?" He sighed, placing one hand on her forehead and one over her heart. "Fine. I will make the attempt." He pursed his lips and growled as he concentrated, sweat beading at his temples. His whole body trembled as he sought to make things right. His bloodshot eyes began to tear as he feared he'd be unable to heal her. "You mustn't leave."

Finally, his hands began to glow, lighting up her skin with the power of a thousand stars. Her swelling went down, her nose righted itself. Her broken bones came back together and her lungs filled with air.

She sprung up, her eyes flying open as she gasped and clutched her chest. Lucifer fell back, exhausted, lying in a pool of sweat.

She slid next to him, still too weak to stand. "You okay?"

"Fine," he panted.

"Wendy?!" Gabriel called as she rushed into the apartment.

"I'm all right," she said as Gabriel dropped to the floor in front of her.

She ran her hands over her, checking for wounds before kissing her and running her hands through her hair. "I'm sorry. I should've told you about--"

"I'm sorry, too. I overreacted. The truth is, I'm pretty sure I'm in love with you."

She wiped away a tear and kissed her again.

"Well, I'm off to bed," Lucifer said, sitting himself up. "Do clean up this mess before the corpses give off a smell."

Gabriel threw her arms around her brother's neck, almost knocking him back down. "Thank you."

"It was nothing." He patted her back and pulled away so he could stand.

"Really. I owe you. Huge."

"I'll keep it in mind. Goodnight." He shuffled off to his room, leaving the two alone among the bodies.

"What the hell happened?"

"Witch hunters," Wendy huffed.

"Ah."

"Did you know Lucifer knew Tituba?"

"Yeah. You didn't?"

She shook her head.

"Oh, yeah. They hung out a few times in the 1690s. He even made a special trip topside when he found out she'd been arrested. Had to *buy* her to get her released. He still feels weird about that. Slavery really pissed him off."

Everything all right? She heard Wyatt in her head.

Fine. Lucifer saved her. I told you he's a good dude. She glanced around at the dead bodies. *Maybe a little messy.*

Chapter 22

Hartley peeked her head into the chapel. The priest had already begun speaking, so she tiptoed in and found a seat at the back of the church where she hoped to go unnoticed. In the pews ahead of her she saw her mother's nurse, a woman she vaguely recognized as being one of her mother's friends that babysat her when she was young, and about thirty people she'd never seen before. The smell of incense made her queasy as she listened to the eulogy, the priest's words hitting harder than she'd expected.

"Gloria was a pillar of her community. From her work at the women's shelter and the soup kitchen to her charitable donations to cancer research, crisis relief, and back-to-school preparedness programs, she was a shining example of what a servant of God should be. Helping others was what gave her joy. When it came to the church, she was one of the most devoted members I've ever seen, leading Bible study, singing in the choir, and hosting fundraisers twice a year to raise money for repairs and maintenance for our beloved church home. No one here will ever forget the fire that gutted this very sanctuary twelve years ago. The city almost had the building condemned. But, Gloria went out, going door-to-door, raising funds to bring us back from the brink. All told, she raised over one point six million dollars. We're only here today because of her love for God and our church family. No one will ever be able to replace Gloria Morales. She will be missed for generations to come." He made the sign of the cross, as did the crowd. Hartley noticed several people crying, including the nurse. The priest himself looked to be getting misty. "At this time, I'd like to invite friends and family to come to the pulpit and say a few words."

Wanda stood, going to the head of the room and smoothing a piece of paper out in front of her. "First, I'd like to thank you all for welcoming me. I didn't know Gloria for very long and when we met, she was already pretty far along in her illness. Still, she'd have moments of clarity. They could last a few days or just a few minutes. In one of those moments, she wrote this letter to all of you. She asked me to read it at her funeral." She cleared her throat and looked down at the page. "To my friends and church family, I love you. You've made my time on this earth easier and less painful. You picked me up when I was down. You gave me strength when I was weak. You helped me see what was broken in me and gave me the courage to right the wrongs that had shattered me. You lifted me up and I have no words for how grateful I am for that. To Father Daniel, your visits have meant the world to me. Most people couldn't stand to see me in this state, but you have been here for me. I am truly blessed to have your prayers, guidance, and friendship. Thank you. And, to my son,"

Hartley's ears perked up, her stomach flipping as she bit her bottom lip.

"My sweet, beautiful baby boy, you may never hear this and that's my fault. I wasn't there for you the way I should have been. I didn't know how to parent a child like you. I was a bad mother. I know that and I'm sorry. I hope that the actions I took in the past were enough to give you some peace of mind. That knowing you're safe, at least from one person who didn't understand you, is of some comfort to you. Even though I didn't get to watch you become the person you were meant to be, or see you fall in love, or even smile without pain in your eyes, I can feel you in my heart every day. I love you more than you'll ever know and I hope that life gives you everything you ask of it.

And, to everyone listening, don't cry for me. Don't grieve what's lost. Instead, love what's in front of you. Be kind, do good works, and love yourselves the way you wish to be loved. I'll see you all again one day. Goodbye."

Hartley covered her mouth as tears rolled down her cheeks.

"Hartley, dear, is that you?" Wanda asked. The crowd turned to look at her.

She wiped her face and sat up straight. "Y-yes."

"Would you like to say something? Everyone, this is Hartley, Gloria's granddaughter."

She was a deer in headlights as they stared. Slowly, she stood, smoothing her charcoal-black Etsuko dress and making her way to the pulpit. She glanced down at the closed casket, breathing a sigh of relief that she didn't actually have to see her mother's dead body. Wanda gave her arm a quick pat before handing her the letter and taking her seat.

"I'm not really sure what to say," Hartley admitted. "I hadn't spoken to Gloria in years. I thought coming here would be easier. I didn't expect to be so emotional." She paused, swallowing hard as she gathered her nerve. "I didn't know her the way all of you did. I grew up being worried about what she thought of me. I was downright afraid if I'm being honest." She blew out a mournful breath. "I don't think I can ever forget how she made me feel as a scared, lonely, queer kid just looking for *one person* to stick up for me and not having that. I don't know that I can ever forgive her for not being what I needed her to be. But, I do think I can come to terms with it now." She wiped the last tear from her face. "I'm ready to move on."

Lucifer sauntered into Gabriel's apartment the morning of the wedding carrying a large envelope. "Sister, I'm glad I caught you."

Gabriel swallowed a bite of pumpkin pie-flavored toaster pastry and crossed her legs, resting her elbows on the island. "You're leaving?"

"I'm having a bit of an existential crisis. Thought I might do some traveling. Would you mind giving this to William and extending my apologies to the happy couple for missing the blessed event?"

She opened the envelope and pulled out the deed, leaving the keys inside. "You bought them a building in Brooklyn?"

"Just a six-story on Dekalb. Nothing overtly pretentious."

"Sixteen million dollars?"

"Fifteen point eight and that money was going to waste just sitting in your account."

"What do you expect them to do with twenty-eight apartments and three commercial spaces?"

"Whatever they like. Michelle's inheritance will run out eventually. Raphael was a surgeon, not a titan of industry.

This gives them security. Options. I'm surprised *you* didn't think of it. What did you get them?"

"I'm paying for the wedding."

"And?"

"Nothing."

"Come now, Gabriel."

She bit her bottom lip and averted her glance. "*And*, a trip to the Moon."

"A *what*?"

"A private company's doing them now."

"How much is that?"

She shifted in her seat. "Eighty-one million."

He raised his eyebrows.

"Each."

He laughed.

"Hey, it is a once-in-a-lifetime experience."

"It would have to be."

She put the page back in the envelope and resealed it. "I'll give them your present."

"Thank you." He turned to go. "I'll be back."

"Lucifer," She got up and walked over to him, giving him a hug and patting his back. "Take care of yourself."

"I always do."

Hartley sat on the edge of the bed staring at the three pills in her palm. *This is it*, she thought. *No going back*. She popped them in her mouth, estrogen, progesterone, and anti-androgen. She took a sip of water and swallowed them down. Now that she was human, her body could change. In a few years, her outside would finally match her inside.

She walked to the window as she tied her hair up in a messy bun, closing it against the cool ocean breeze that gave her chills. She watched the sunlight glisten on the waves as they crashed against the beach and admired the wispy clouds that floated in the havelock sky.

She left Oliver in bed while she went to the kitchen to make breakfast. She had never been a good cook, but she'd recently discovered she could make anything that came in a tube. So, she set the oven to three hundred and fifty degrees, banged a package of cinnamon rolls on the counter, and opened it, placing the icing cup on the stove and separating the rolls of dough onto the sheet pan. She washed her hands, put the pan in the oven, and set the timer. She sat at the bar, taking her phone from the charger and smiling. Her life was blissfully normal and for the first time maybe ever, she didn't feel afraid.

She went into her texts and found Allydia's number. Her cat leaped into her lap and then to the counter, her tail smacking Hartley in the face. She giggled and typed the words, *Thank you*. She hit 'send' and put the phone down before getting the cat's food in her bowl and again sitting, resting her cheek on her hand as she allowed herself to feel something she'd never dreamed was in her reach...happiness.

Allydia texted back, *You're most welcome* and put her phone down on the charger in her kitchen as Navid came in to meet her.

"That's a nice dress," he commented. "What are you all gussied up for?"

"A wedding." She glared at the suitcase in his hand. "What's this?"

"Just packin' up the few things I bought while I was here."

"You're leaving?"

"Yeah, it's about time I get back to work. We can't all be independently wealthy."

She leaned on the counter. "I've funded your savings and current accounts to eighty-five thousand pounds and deposited twenty million dollars into a Swiss account under your name."

He blinked and shook his head. "You what?"

"I must have forgotten to mention it. I would have put more in your UK accounts, but they're only insured up to--"

"You didn't have to do that."

She squinted for a second. "Of course I did. What's the point of having money if not to take care of people?"

"Thank you, but recent events aside, I can actually take care of myself."

"I'm sure you can. It's not an insult." She walked past him and made her way to her bedroom where she opened a drawer full of various types of jewelry. He followed her, standing in the doorway as she retrieved a diamond tennis bracelet and carefully put it on her wrist.

"I can't take your money. It makes me feel a bit like a child."

"You *are* my child," she asserted as she placed diamond studs in her ears. "In a way. If you never touch the money, it won't hurt my feelings. It's there in case you need it and that gives me peace of mind. When are you going?"

"In the morning. Flight leaves at ten."

"You should come to the wedding, then. Do you have a suit? Let's buy you a suit."

"Whose wedding is it?"

"Wyatt's son's. And his niece's, sort of."

"Oh, that's, um…"

"They're not related by blood. Wyatt and the bride's uncle are both angels."

"Whew, I was worried I'd stumbled onto something I'd be better off not knowin'. You know, I don't think you ever told me which angel your man is."

"Oh, he's Barachiel, Protector of Humanity."

"Really?"

"Yes. Why do you say 'really' like that?"

"Just strikes me as odd, guardian angel takin' up with the queen of vampires. How'd you manage it?"

She clicked her tongue and tossed her hair over her shoulder. "Persistence."

"Will there be other angels there?"

"Yes. Uriel who goes by Valerie, and Gabriel, of course." She noticed him cross his arms at the sound of her name. "She'll be there with her girlfriend, the witch that turned me back. Will that make you uncomfortable?"

"No," he said, feigning a casual tone.

She didn't quite believe him but moved on. "Good. Michelle, the bride, is human as is Uriel's husband, Malik. Uriel and Malik have adopted Will and Michelle's daughter, Sinclair, who's part Nephilim and part vampire. Because she was born and not bitten, she retains her vampire nature. I am uneasy about it, but I've spoken to Gabriel and she claims the girl is a danger to no one. Something about the way she said it, though."

He stared, wide-eyed, his concern obvious.

"No harm will come to you, I promise."

"You sure about that?"

She used her finger to make a cross over her heart.

He snickered.

"Now, let's go get you a suit. We'll have to hurry. We have a plane to catch."

"A plane? Where is this wedding?"

Chapter 23

"It feels like it's been a lifetime since I've been here," Will said as Wyatt fixed his tie. Standing in his childhood bedroom in Southport, he tried to push the memories of the last time he was there from his mind, but they haunted his thoughts like malevolent spirits, ready to send him into a meltdown at any moment. Beating the pizza guy half to death, what he'd done to his father...the wolves. He was feeling unsteady, but he kept himself together. It was important to Michelle that they get married in the place where they'd first said 'I love you', so he pushed through his demons. *Anything* to make her happy.

"It kind of was," Wyatt teased, seeing how uneasy his son was and attempting to lighten his mood. "I mean, you did die."

He snorted.

"You sure you're ready for this?"

"Honestly? She's the *only* thing I'm sure about. Like, in life."

He gave a quiet smile as he finished adjusting the tie and straightened his own.

"What?"

"Nothing, just," He finished with his tie and picked up his jacket. "That's exactly how I felt when I married your mother."

"You still miss her?"

"I think part of me always will." He felt himself getting emotional, so he took a deep breath as he put on the jacket, not wanting to ruin his son's day. "She'd be really proud of you."

"You think so?"

"Are you kidding? Michelle's way out of your league. If your mom was here, she'd run up to the altar and high-five you as soon as you said, 'I do'."

Will burst out laughing. "Just because you're right, doesn't mean you have to be rude."

He laughed.

"So, do you have any advice?"

"Marriage advice?" He cringed and crossed his arms as he thought. "Well, I guess I'd say, don't panic when you argue, because you *will* argue. A lot. It's normal. What you have to do is stay on topic, never insult her, and remember that at the end of the day, what you're really fighting for is the health of your relationship. Put that first and everything else will fall into place. Easier said than done, but do your best to keep it in mind."

"That's solid advice."

"I'm wise beyond my years," Wyatt joked.

"Aren't you really, like, two-hundred-thousand years old?"

He laughed again. "Probably. I'd have to ask Gabriel for an exact number."

"It's not that hard to figure out. You were created to protect people and people, as we know them, didn't exist until--"

He shook his head. "All right, smart-ass." He handed Will his jacket and patted him on the shoulder. "Let's get you married."

Locked away in Wyatt's old bedroom, out of sight from her fiance's prying eyes, Michelle let Gabriel help her with her makeup. There was no way she was letting Will see her before she walked down the aisle. Yes, it was superstitious, but with her luck, she wasn't taking any chances.

As the angel applied a small amount of highlighter to her cheekbones, Michelle wondered something. "Does it feel ridiculous that you had to get online-ordained to perform the ceremony, given who you are?"

"A little," she admitted.

"My uncle called you 'the highest authority on Earth'. Seems silly you need a piece of paper to prove you can do something."

"A piece of paper like a marriage license?" she teased.

She grinned. "Haha."

She put the brush down and picked up the mascara. "Look up."

She did as she was told and Gabriel applied a final coat to her long lashes.

"Just so you know, I'm not an authority on anything. I'm an errand boy. I relay messages. That's really it." She put the tube down and stood, waving her hand for Michelle to do the same, which she did. She held the Cinderella-like dress open for her to step into and pulled it up around her.

"You're more than that. You're like a second mother to me."

"Well, that's terrifying. You know I'm not a role model, right?"

"I hate to break it to you, but you don't get to decide how I perceive you."

She bit her tongue. "Fair enough." She zipped her up and stood her in front of the mirror.

"Holy crap." She lit up as she admired the dress, its lace bodice with cap sleeves and plunging neckline accentuated her body perfectly and the full skirt made entirely from fairy-tale 3D lace made to look like leaves was hyper-dramatic, just as she'd requested. She'd never seen herself as beautiful but now, staring at her reflection as Gabriel added a few more bobby pins to her sparkling crystal tiara to keep it firmly in place, she was floored by how stunning she was.

"So weird when hot girls don't know they're hot," Gabriel commented.

"Hey," She turned to look at her. "I know you don't need to hear it, but thank you. None of this would be happening if not for you. I don't just mean the wedding. I mean any of it. If you hadn't sent me here…" She stopped, choking back tears, and fanning her face.

"Okay, okay. Don't ruin your makeup getting all up in your feelings already. I'm not doing that shit again." She got a tissue from the makeup bag and dabbed it under her friend's eyes.

She took the tissue and blew out a calming breath.
"Better?"

She nodded. "I mean it, though. You gave me a whole family when I'd lost mine. I'll always be grateful for that. I love you." She hugged her, careful not to let her freshly made-up face touch Gabriel's rose-red dress.

"I love you, too, girl." She hugged her back, chewing on her lip as she stifled her own worried tears. "I really do."

Gabriel knelt in front of Sinclair to hand her the white wicker basket of rose petals and smoothed back a hair that had strayed out from underneath her crystal headband. She adjusted the girl's shoe that had somehow slipped off in the back and when she was finished, she brushed the curls from her shoulders, flashing a half-hearted smile. "Beautiful as always."

"Gabriel,"

"Hmm?"

"Grandpa was right. You should take a break. You deserve it."

"That's kind of you to say, but--"

"Gabriel," she touched her cheek. "You're doing a good job."

Her eyes swelled with tears as Sinclair kissed her cheek and threw her arms around her neck. She held her for a few seconds as she got her emotions in check.

"Are you ready, baby?" Michelle asked as she met them at the edge of the forest.

"Ready, Mommy!" she beamed, handing Gabriel a tissue she pulled from her left shoe.

Gabriel blotted her damp cheeks and held back a chuckle as she stood.

The bride bent down and pointed to the white linen runner that stretched from where they stood to the clearing in front of the creek. "Just follow that cloth all the way to the end. When you get to Daddy, sit down with Malik and Valerie, okay?"

"I got it, Mommy." She skipped down the path lit by twinkly lights that covered every tree on either side.

"Are you sure she'll be all right? The sun's going down and it's a long way to the wedding."

Gabriel scoffed. "Strongest creature on Earth, remember? Nothing's gonna fuck with her out here."

"Okay." She took a deep breath and blew it out slowly as she steadied her nerves.

"Didn't you take public speaking in school?"

"Yeah."

"There are only seven people down there."

"That's not what I'm nervous about and you know it."

Gabriel shot her a condescending glare.

"I wish you could tell me, you know, for sure."

"Hey," Gabriel smiled. "I don't need superpowers to be able to tell that that boy loves you."

"What if--"

"No 'what if's'."

"But--"

"A couple of years ago, he was about five and I brought him as a present his own laptop. B hadn't let him on the internet yet because he'd read like, *all* the parenting books and thought it was too soon." She rolled her eyes. "So, I talked him into letting me give it to him, which took some arm twisting, but I mean, come on. The kid's a genius. It would have been cruel to stifle him, right? So, he opens the box and I get it all plugged in and set up and I'm telling you, his face lit up like a goddamn Christmas tree. He did everything on that computer from that day on. School, shopping, the occasional trolling of politicians on social media. It was his link to the outside world. It meant everything to him."

"That's cute, but what does it have to do with anything?"

"Because, dummy, he looks at you the same way he looked at that laptop for the first time, with hope and excitement. When you talk, he hangs on every word like he might fall off a cliff. When you leave the room, for a split second, I can see a little twinge of sadness on his face. Will loves you. The only thing you have to worry about is making sure you always remember that. Golden rule that shit."

"What?"

"Marriage. Just like anything else, it works like magic. Do unto him as you'd have him do unto you."

"Ah," she laughed.

"I didn't mean it that way, filthy." She waved her hands in front of herself to try to get the image out of her head.

"It works that way, too, though."

She gagged. "You're grossing me out now."

The music started, "Once Upon A Time...Storybook Love", wafting through the trees on the PA system Gabriel had installed, run by the DJ who'd set up just out of sight of the actual ceremony.

"I guess it's time," Michelle said, grinning from ear to ear.

"All right, girl. Go get your man."

Chapter 24

The setting sun cast a rosy hue through the trees as Will stood at the altar, his skin glowing under the lights that twinkled all around him, in the trees and cascading down from the Spanish Dress and white rose-covered arbor. In front of him, the aisle ran deep into the woods. On one side sat Malik, Valerie, and Wendy. On the other, his father, Allydia, and Navid, who he'd never met, but seemed like a nice enough guy. Behind him, the sound of the rushing creek filled the air. He squeezed his hands together in front of him, the anticipation driving him crazy. As beautiful as this all was, he just wanted to be married. He couldn't wait to make Michelle his wife. He only hoped he would always do right by her.

Allydia could see the torment Wyatt was trying to hide in his eyes. She held his hand and rubbed his arm. She remembered the last time they were in this place, Wyatt cradling Will's limp body in the grass as he cried and feeling helpless as she had no way of easing his pain. "Is it hard to be back here?"

"A little." He kissed her hand, trying to ignore the memories that flashed in his mind. "A little."

"He looks happy."

Wyatt smiled. "He does, doesn't he?"

"It really is beautiful out here."

"It can be."

Overhead, they heard one song fade out and another begin, Haley Reinhart's version of "Can't Help Falling In Love". The small crowd turned to see Sinclair skipping down the aisle, tossing red and white rose petals from a basket, her face lit up with a smile that could melt the coldest of hearts. She bounced up to Will. "Happy wedding, Daddy!"

"Thank you, sweetie," he giggled. She took her seat on Valerie's lap as Gabriel made her way to the altar, standing behind Will and facing the crowd. Finally, emerging from the trees like a fairy princess, Michelle made her entrance. Will's knees went weak as his heart raced, the sight of her giving him life. He caught himself, having to take a step back so he wouldn't fall as he whispered to himself, "I am *not* good enough for her."

She stepped to the altar, taking Will's hand as the couple faced their officiant.

Gabriel took the bride's bouquet and cleared her throat as the music stopped. "We are gathered here today to celebrate the joining of William Ross Sinclair and Michelle Narissa Iha in Holy Matrimony. Who gives this woman to be married to this man?"

Sinclair raised her hand. "I do!"

They all laughed as Gabriel gave her a wink and continued. "I won't ask if anyone objects because I already know that no one does. So, at this time, the couple will make their vows. Michelle."

She nodded, holding tightly to Will's hands. "There was a time when I didn't think I'd ever love anyone. I was cynical. Love was a pipe dream, and risky, and I wasn't even sure if I wanted it. But, you wrecking-balled my walls down with a *look*. I fell so hard, I thought I might break something. I am so stupid in love with you, the thought of being without you makes me want to die. So, I will spend every day making sure you never doubt it. I love you, Will, and you will *always* have me."

He kissed her hands and choked back tears as he drew in a breath, looking down at her and trying to maintain his balance. "Michelle, I could go on and on forever about how perfect and amazing you are and how unbelievably lucky I am because, *my God*, I am lucky. I could tell you all the things I'll do to make you happy because you deserve everything. I could make promises I have no idea if I'll be able to keep. I could recite poetry or sing a song, although, I don't think anyone wants to hear that."

A burst of laughter came from the crowd.

"But, what it all boils down to is that I love you. *I love you* and for the rest of my life and every life after, that will always be true."

Gabriel fanned her eyes. "You kids. All right, Will, repeat after me. With this ring, I thee wed."

He took the diamond infinity band from his pocket and placed it on her finger. "With this ring, I thee wed."

Gabriel handed Michelle Will's ring. "Michelle, repeat after me. With this ring, I thee wed."

She put the white gold band on his finger. "With this ring, I thee wed."

"Awesome. By the power vested in me by I'mOrdained.com, the state of Indiana, and God Him-freakin'-self, I now pronounce you husband and wife. Go ahead and kiss."

"Crash Into Me" played over the speakers as Will took his new wife's face in his hands and kissed her, so lost in the moment he didn't hear the guests' applause.

A proud smile fell on Wyatt's face as he brushed away a single tear. Allydia put her hand on his knee and as he held it, she rested her head on his shoulder. "They're very sweet. I'm glad I didn't kill them."

He laughed, patting the back of her hand.

"Daddy!" Sinclair called from her seat, breaking the trance. Will pulled away as he and Michelle turned to look at their beaming daughter, Gabriel handing back Michelle's bouquet.

"Yeah, sweetie?"

"Is it over? I'm starving."

He laughed, "Yeah, sweetie, it's over."

"Great!" She hopped down and darted back into the woods on her way to the reception Gabriel had set up in Wyatt's old backyard. The bride and groom followed, holding hands and giggling as they disappeared beyond the trees.

Wendy got up to meet Gabriel at the altar, plucking a rose from the arbor and handing it to her. "They're cute together, huh?"

"Yeah. I just wish I didn't have to hear every carnal thought she had about him."

She covered her mouth and snickered.

"You laugh, but it legit makes me nauseous. There are things an aunt isn't supposed to know about her nephew. It's not right."

She took her hand away and held it to her stomach as she cracked up.

"I'm glad my suffering amuses you."

"It really does. I'm sorry," She calmed herself. "I'm sorry, it must be terrible." She leaned in to whisper in her ear. "Do you think we could sneak away for a while? I'm not wearing anything under this dress. Maybe we could replace those dirty thoughts with--"

"Yep." She took her hand and led her into the woods.

Navid watched them leave, the last of the guests still at the clearing. He bowed his head as he followed the aisle into the forest, bitter acceptance settling in his gut as he reminded himself that she was an angel of God and he was just a man, undeserving but blessed to have been in her presence at all.

Sinclair sat quietly, devouring her second piece of cake while the adults gathered on the dance floor, chit-chatting while they waited for the music to start. With no warning, Michelle hurried to the edge of the smooth wood platform and flung her bouquet into the crowd. It hit Allydia in the chest, causing her to grasp it on instinct. The other guests clapped as she examined her prize.

"These are lovely. I'll just go inside and put them in some water." She gave Wyatt a quick peck on the cheek before heading toward the house. They exchanged smiles and waves as she went in through the back door.

"So," Navid said, taking his ancestor's place next to Wyatt and folding his arms. "You're an angel, yeah?"

"Apparently."

"And, what does that mean, exactly?"

He gave him a puzzled glare. "What do you mean?"

"Well, you have angel business, right? Savin' the world and whatnot."

"Occasionally."

"And, that takes priority, yeah? I mean, God's will be done and all that."

"I guess."

"So, what's that mean for her?"

"Allydia?"

"Yeah, mate. She's human now. She can't be gettin' mixed up in whatever antics you and your angel buddies got goin' on at any given time. So, tell me, *Barachiel*, what exactly are your intentions with my gran?"

Wyatt was silent for a moment before erupting in laughter.

Navid squinted, scrunching his brow, his face stern.

Wyatt could see the seriousness on the man's face and went quiet. He tried, but after a few seconds, he couldn't hold back any longer. He put his hand to his chest and bowled over in a fit of laughter, wiping away tears as he patted Navid on the back.

Finally, the Death Cab For Cutie version of "Earth Angel" began to play, the crowd dispersing as Will and Michelle took the floor for their first dance as husband and wife.

Navid sat down and took a sip of champagne as Gabriel walked over to stand next to Wyatt. She looked up at him, a wide smile covering her face.

"What?" he asked.

"You feel that, right?"

"Feel what?"

She coyly averted her glance. "Well, I don't want to scare you."

He chuckled. "What?"

She leaned in, speaking in hushed tones as if she were telling him a secret. "Don't freak out, but," She looked around as he leaned in closer. "You're happy."

He laughed and let out a sigh. "I think you're right."

"Um, duh."

"What about you? That whole Wendy thing get resolved?"

"Oh, yeah. We made up…a bunch of times. We just made up again in the woods about half an hour ago."

He squeezed his eyes shut and shook his head. "Unnecessary."

She giggled.

"So, you're good? Everything's right with the world?"

She glanced over to see Wendy holding out a leaf in front of Sinclair who watched in awe as the witch waved her hand over it, changing its red autumn coloring back to green. She shifted her gaze back to her brother and smiled. "For the most part."

"Anything you need help with?"

She took his arm and watched the couple dance, putting her head on his shoulder as she calmed her nerves. "I'll keep you posted."

Chapter 25

The house was dark, the only light coming in through the draped windows. The living room was cold, the heat having never been turned on with the changing of the season. Bills and advertisements piled at the threshold under the mail slot as the phone on the charger rang to no answer. The call went to voicemail and the room again was silent. In the corner, the Gothic iron birdcage hung from the ceiling, left undisturbed for weeks. The crow inside lay still on the newspaper-lined bottom, dead from dehydration.

Lying stiff on the loop pile carpet, Julia's body rested where she'd fallen, overcome with pain and exhaustion. The life had left her long before, but something in her remained, growing...evolving.

The corpse's belly had swollen to twice its normal size and now, as night fell over the dead witch's home, the stretched skin began to move as if something were underneath, fighting its way out. After a few moments, the skin and muscle tore open, dozens of snakes bursting forth from the cavity. A tar-like substance followed, oozing out onto the floor as the overpowering stench of sulfur escaped the body, filling the room with its noxious odor.

The body's glassy stare seemed purposefully fixed on the ceiling above, as if she'd known. Even the dead were terrified of what was to come.

The End

The Complete Seventh Day Series

Seraphim
Nephilim
Elohim
Cain
Alukah
Coven
Sinclair

Printed in Great Britain
by Amazon